GOTTERDAMMERUNG

Hitler moved with the shuffling steps of an old man, his right arm trembling, eyes vacuous, lips pale. He moved down the corridor followed by the last of the royal retainers, stopping before the entrance to his small rooms. Turning, he looked at the faces of those left out of the millions that had so recently worshipped at his altar of the greater German Reich.

Casca stood silently as the Führer shook the hands of the men and patted the cheeks of the women.

"This man," he said, touching Casca's sleeve, "does not exist. You have never seen him. *He has never been here*. He must be left to go his way without delay or hindrance. Do you understand?"

CASCA:

PANZER SOLDIER

#4

BARRY SADLER

ACE CHARTER BOOKS, NEW YORK

CASCA #4: PANZER SOLDIER

An Ace Charter Original

ISBN: 0-441-09222-5

First Ace Charter Printing: September 1980
Sixth Ace Charter Printing: December 1982

Published simultaneously in Canada

Manufactured in the United States of America

Ace Books, 200 Madison Avenue, New York, New York 10016

PROLOGUE

Berlin, an industrious modern city filled with busy laughing people, full of the good-natured German *Gemütlichkeit*. They worked hard, sang songs and were proud of their city and its place in the world. Modern new buildings rose at every corner, but underneath the new hills that rose from the piled up rubble of WW II lay the ruins of an entire way of life, built on hate and fear.

The Germans he'd met here this day had little resemblance to those that had slaughtered millions in the name of racial purity. But in the back of his mind, he wondered how much of the beast still lay in the hearts of these happy hard working people. He had been at Auschwitz and had seen the death machine that had sent millions of Jews and others considered to be subhuman, to their deaths. The feeling still walked with him. It was hard to shake.

He was in Berlin for a medical seminar at the

University. He felt a sense of regret for coming. He had thought he was too modern to hold grudge against a whole people for what had happened when he was a child living in another country across the ocean. He walked by the wall separating east from west. Guard towers were easily spotted along the wall, manned by men with machine guns. On one of the walls he saw scribbled the words "Heil Hitler" in white paint. He felt an odd sense of satisfaction that there were still some Nazis around. Maybe it made the rest more believable. He sat at a table at a sidewalk restaurant and listened to the music from the stereo inside. He admired the well dressed women, with long legs and fair hair. Some of the most beautiful women in the world could be found here.

Still, it wasn't difficult to let his imagination run free and see the streets change to one filled with swastika flags, and ranks of marching jackbooted soldiers and SS passing in review, to the strains of the SS anthem, or *Deutschland Über Alles*. The hammering of boots slamming down as thousands of people, eyes raised, arms in a salute, millions of them crowding the sidewalks, held back by members of the *Sturm Abteilung* detachments. Again and again he could hear them in his mind, crying out in impassioned voices, crying in cadence as their messiah passed by in a Mercedes *Heil Hitler, Heil Hitler*.

Goldman ran his hands over his face to wipe out the images. God, has it been such a short time since the madness? A waiter, smiling, interrupted his thoughts; had Goldman ordered a bottle of good

German pilsner? Trying to collect himself back from a past he had never experienced, except through films and the words of others, was difficult. He was a Jew and here was the capitol city of a nation that had once dedicated itself to the destruction of his race and religion. A deep voice spoke at his shoulder in good German, *"Guten abend Herr Doktor; wie geht es ihnen?"* Goldman froze. Turning slowly, he looked at his visitor. A scarred face smiled down at him. "May I join you, Doctor?" Goldman merely nodded permission. His guest settled himself into the chair opposite and ordered a Steinhaer from the waiter. "Well, Doctor, it seems that destiny has once again made our paths cross; what brings you to Berlin?"

Goldman explained the conference. His guest smiled, understanding.

"Yes, of course there is always that, but from the look on your face, when I saw you sitting here, I would guess there is another reason. It's a strange city isn't it, so full of life now, and gaiety. Ahhh, but you should have been here in '34 or '35, it was even more fascinating and beautiful than now."

Goldman finally gained control. "Casca, what are you doing here, did you follow me?"

The scar-faced man laughed. "No, good doctor, our meeting was strictly coincidence, but I must admit, I have thought often of you since our last meeting at your lovely home in Boston. What was it? Two years ago? I lose track of time." He laughed at his own joke and repeated, more for himself than anyone else, "Lose track of time."

Goldman interrupted him and repeated his question, "Why are you here?"

Casca answered slowly, "First, call me Carl; Carl Langer. It's the name I have become used to while in Germany. I used it for a long time in the war years."

Goldman hesitated before he spoke again. "You mean you fought for the Nazis?"

Langer smiled gently. "Don't get excited, Herr Doktor, it's not what you might think, and I'm here for the same reason you are, perhaps, though, in a slightly different way. I was here when it all ended; the Reich, I mean. It was a much different place than you see now. Would you like to hear the rest of the story of how I came to be in Berlin on April 30, 1945?"

Goldman looked at him questioningly and ran his fingers through his graying hair. "That was the day Hitler committed suicide, wasn't it?"

Langer chuckled in a manner of his own. "Come, let's walk." Langer paid for the drinks and the two walked out on the streets. Langer kept up a running dialogue of the grace and beauty of the city before the war, the singing and the parties and a happy people full of life. A life that was soon to end in the greatest conflict the world had ever known.

As Goldman walked with Langer, he was caught up once again in whatever power this man had over him, to draw him back into the past, to actually be there, to feel what he felt and know the reality of another existence.

"You know, Doctor, the real war was fought on the Russian front. That's where the big battles were. Hitler always considered the Russians to be

4

his greatest threat, and rightly so. You think you saw some horrible things when we were in Vietnam? What you experienced there was nothing to what took place on the eastern front.

The eastern front. He repeated the words over and over until he felt the sounds of trains rolling over the rails. *"Clack! clack! clack!"* the city faded from his eyes. All he heard was the rattling of train wheels rolling through the night.

CHAPTER ONE

The smooth-cheeked young Vikings of the Greater German Reich raised their voices, full of life and eagerness for the great adventure they were fortunate enough to be taking part in.

"*Die fahne hoch, die reihen fest geschlossen. . .*" The "Horst Wessel Leid," the song of the Nazi Storm Troops, resounded throughout the smoky interior of the train. The rattling of the wheels became the timekeeper for the group of novices going to join the 1st SS Panzer Regiment being reoutfitted outside of Kharkov. The train began to pick up speed after they transferred over to captured Russian engines and cars in order to use the narrower, Soviet-gauge tracks.

Kharkov was still two days away. The mixed bag of Luftwaffe, Wehrmacht and SS men were having

a good time. It would be tough shit when they finally got face to face with Ivan, now that they were
bringing the long-barrelled Mark V Panther tanks,
Germany's answer to the Soviet T-34.

RECRUITS. . .

The older-looking *Feldwebel* huddled in his
camouflaged field jacket. The soft M-43 cap bore a
Deathshead emblem, often causing novices to con-
fuse the tankers with the SS, the only difference
being the tanker's skull had no lower jawbone. He
shifted the MP-40 submachine gun to a more handy
position nearer the window and lit a Turkish
cigarette, sucking the acrid yellow fumes back up
into his nostrils, inhaling deeply and letting the biting smoke reach into his lungs.

Watching the young men, he thought how lucky
for them it was dark so that they could not see the
thousands of German graves standing in precise
military rows like a small white forest of German
crosses, reaching for kilometers.

He had come this way twice, once on the way to
Moscow and once when the Siberian divisions
pushed them back with the T-34s, which had come
into the battle unpainted, just off the assembly lines
from Moscow factories. Butting his smoke on the
sole of his boot, he was thankful he wasn't stuck
with a pair of jack boots. Those damn hobnails
caused as many casualties as the Russians did, by
letting the cold run directly into the fee t, causing
frostbite.

"*SA marshiert, in ruhig festen shritt* . . ." It's a
good marching song, but they'll learn it takes more
than that soon enough. The younger men, for their

7

part, left the dour-looking *Feldwebel* alone. Piss on him if he was a wet blanket. None, however, had the nerve to tell him so. The scarred face along with the "IK I," Iron Cross first class would have been indicators enough, but a silver tanker's badge showed over fifty tank engagements.

The youngsters left *Die Alte,* the old one, alone. For them, anyone near or over thirty classified for that appellation. The man whose paybook and documents permitting travel said he was one Carl Langer merely watched the young ones, slightly amused at their antics and histrionics. The few other old soldiers sat silently or played cards among themselves. They knew what waited at the end of the line.

Back into the cauldron. There death walked at every man's shoulder, quick sudden death if you were lucky, or a cartridge casing hammered into the back of the neck by the NKVD; Asiatic smiling faces that laughed beneath the green cross emblem that gave them even more power than the Gestapo, if you were unlucky.

Moving the steel helmet strapped in the regulation manner to the back of his pack, he reached in and took out a bottle of prewar French Calvados. Taking a long pull, he found the sweet burning served to add an additional sense of dullness to his mind and made the waiting easier. A droning overhead stopped his breath for a moment. From the sound, it was moving east, probably Stukas going in support of the hedgehog past the Oka River near Mtsensk.

The droning lessened the enthusiasm of the

young heroes, and for some the bitter coppery taste of fear came into their mouths with the realization they were not going to be strafed or bombed. The voices became even louder and the laughter more forced.

A grizzled veteran of the Crimean campaign, as shown by the brass Krim shield on his right arm, settled into the seat opposite Langer.

Casting a questioning glance at Langer's bottle, he licked his lips. Langer handed the bottle over with a shrug. The *Stabsgefreiter* took a pull—not too large—and handed the precious fluid back to its owner. He knew how rare such things would be in Russia. Looking at the tank patch . . . "Panzerman?"

Langer nodded and put the bottle back into his pack. The corporal lit a smoke and leaned back, his hands showing severe burn scars. He looked at them forgetting whose hands they were . . .

"*Stabsgefreiter* Alfons Kunik at your service, and thanks for the drink."

Langer nodded again. Kunik pointed at the youngsters with a wave of his hand. "It won't be like France, no short sweet summer campaign, then wine and women. Russia will teach them a new tune to sing. The young always go to war singing and are brought back the same way—with singing at their funerals, where their families can be proud that their sons have been so fortunate to die for the Fatherland and the Führer." He spat on the floor. A quick fleeting trace of fear sparked in his eyes. He had forgotten this kind of talk could get a bullet through the neck if the man he was talking to was a party member or belonged to the SD, *Sicherheits-dienst,* security service.

Langer merely grunted and shifted his ass to a more comfortable position. He leaned his head against the glass window, enjoying the cool feel where it pressed against his skin.

Kunik shifted his Kar-98 rifle to between his legs and watched his companion go to sleep, rocking gently with the swaying of the train. He gave the man a good once over and nodded in approval . . . Tough-looking bastard, and he was then making use of sleep, in short supply here. The youngsters settled down and dozed off shortly before midnight. Langer woke several times when a sound or strange movement of the train occurred. Taking a quick glance to see if all was well, he went back to sleep.

In the car ahead, which the officers had appropriated for themselves, a major with oakleaves to the Knight's Cross was just getting the silk panties off a *Blitzmädel,* a rosy-cheeked nineteen-year-old girl, going to Kharkov to serve as a radio operator for Field Marshal Manstein's Army Group South. The Knight's Cross had done it again. The major gloated over how much patriotic ass a piece of cheap metal could get.

Three times the train was switched to side tracks while the rails in front were repaired. Partisan activity was becoming more and more of a problem. Daylight brought the first signs of the destruction of the war; whole cities and villages gutted and the odor of decay reaching them from the mass graves alongside the tracks.

The *Blitzmädel* was unassed, so to speak, at Kharkov along with most of the recruits, and the train moved on with its cargo of steel dinosaurs another 50 kilometers, where they were unloaded and the crews assembled to drive them to the staging areas where they would be assigned to the 9th Panzer Army for the attack to straighten out the huge inward bulge where seven Russian armies had pushed their way 100 kilometers deep and 150 kilometers wide. In this group was the Elite 6th Guards Army and the 1st Tank Army, almost completely outfitted with T-34s. Kluge's 9th Army would drive south to join with von Manstein's 4th Panzer Army in a pincer movement which they hoped would cut off the seven Russian armies from their logistical support. They would meet at Kursk. Other pincers would drive 50 kilometers behind them and link up between Shchigiry and Tim cutting the only two rail links that could supply the Soviets at two points and provide them with a buffer against counterattacks in force until they had eliminated the Russians in a trap.

Langer moved through the confusion and smoke of the railhead swinging his pack to his shoulders and settling the mpi comfortably across his chest. He moved to the flatcar carrying his tank, reporting to a Hauptman of the 26th Panzer Regiment.

The captain, a tough-looking pro, stuck out his hand. "It's good to see you again, Langer, and knock the tin soldier shit off. We have work to do. Get the drivers in ranks for me and anyone else coming in as replacements in ranks behind them. I

11

want to get these vehicles off this train before a flight of Russian pigeons decides to shit all over them."

Langer nodded and moved to follow orders. Heidemann was a good officer. He bellowed, "Twenty-sixth Panzer here. Replacements in the rear rank stand to."

Magically, out of the confusion of hundreds of men, those who belonged found their way and stood rigidly until Heidemann gave them at ease. Looking them over, he saw several faces he knew well. Most were young confused faces that would grow old before the month was out.

"Those of you who are driving, board your tanks and start engines. Any which do not start will be left behind and you will bring them up later. Those joining the infantry support sections will hitch rides with drivers. You have fifteen minutes to get your tanks off the flatcars and in formation." Then, turning to Langer, "You may dismiss them, Sergeant."

"All right. You heard the man. Hop to it. Section dismissed."

Forty steel leviathans started their engines with the rumbling that only armor has and in the allotted time were in columns. They left the railhead and headed northeast to their division HQ, going for a distance down the tracks of the rail before turning off. The youngsters were silent, looking at the rows of partisans hung from the telegraph poles like obscene fruit. Old-timers hardly noticed. This was Russia.

Two hours' march on the dirt roads left all covered with yellow dust clogging the nostrils and caking everything. A distant rumble reached them from the northeast and columns of black smoke rose thousands of feet into the clear sky. Heidemann, who had chosen to ride with Langer, commented, "Looks like Ivan is giving Orel a pasting today." The smoke was visible all the way to Kromy, but not the sounds of the dying of the hundreds of men disappearing as bomb blasts atomized them, or when fuel tanks blew and turned those near them into cinders, leaving only black charred cadavers with pieces of bone sticking out to show that here had once been men. Long live the Fatherland.

Langer's forty-five-ton tank ran over the already flattened corpses of a horse and rider that had been there since the last of the month. Heidemann tapped Langer on the shoulder with his foot from his perch in the turret. Two taps meant stop. The tanks died, letting the engines idle. They were only six kilometers from Kromy.

Taking his binoculars, the captain scanned the countryside. A tap from his foot on the right shoulder and Langer headed to the right down into a small valley where the rest of the division was encamped, waiting to paint and outfit the tanks.

Rumbling in, the drivers automatically spaced the Panzers out in a staggered line to present less of a target to strafing aircraft and leaped out of the hatches to await further orders. The recruits stood in a lump as all recruits do until an *Oberfeldwebel* rushed to them screaming and getting them into some semblance of order, then quickly marched them off for processing.

"Langer, you and the others stay with your tanks.

13

Your crews will join you shortly. As I said, I'm glad to have you back. There are not so many of us as when you left. I'm glad you were sent to the training regiment. We will talk later." Turning, he left the drivers to their own devices, which meant lighting up or chewing on black bread and washing it down with tepid water from their canteens, until their crews showed up and identified themselves.

All had the look of tough men who had seen Ivan's ass on the run too many times to be frightened when they saw him coming at them. They were the victors of Operation Barbarossa, which had driven to the gates of Moscow and left three million Russians dead or in the bag.

Gerfreiter Stefan Carrel, driver, came over smiling, his face thinner than when last they met, but the twinkle of basic good humor never far behind. Tagging along was Gus Beidemann, who resembled a Panzer more than he did a man; a rumbling, square-jawed, square-bodied devil who could gulp Russian vodka faster than a distillery could produce it and still load and fire twice as fast as any man in the regiment. He slapped a gentle paw against Langer's back, nearly knocking him down.

"Well, you dumb son of a bitch, what the hell are you doing back here? Didn't you have enough sense to run off to Sweden while you were in school? Christ, I thought we taught you better than that. But no matter, you're back and we love you, you delicate little flower."

Pohlman was next, the ever-present square-bowed pipe stuck firmly between his teeth. Pleased, Langer hugged him. "Hello, Teacher. Have you

14

taken care of these devils properly?"

Pohlman smiled gently and spoke in the manner of a school teacher, which was precisely what he had been in Cologne. The gentleness of his attitude had nothing to do with the effectiveness he had shown in combat, whether with tanks or the wood-handled, short-bladed close-combat knife stuck in his boot top.

Taking his pipe out, he spat a loose piece of tobacco on the ground and tapped the bowl of the pipe against the sole of his boot.

"No, Carl, I am afraid there is no hope for these cretinous fecal encephalos."

"What the hell's a fecal wachmacallit, you over-educated molester of schoolchildren?"

"A fecal encephalo means shit brain, shit brain."

Beidemann grinned. "That's okay then. For a second, I thought he was insulting us."

Carl looked at the youngster standing behind Pohlman, a nice young man like one of those posters for the *Hitler Jugend*, blond-haired, blue-eyed, with a face that would make angels weep for envy. If he lived, he would give the girls their fair share of heartbreaks; if he lived or went home in one piece, neither of which was very likely.

"Who's this, Teacher?"

"Our new pup. He's our new hull gunner and radio operator. Felix bought it."

Another gone. Nothing else could be said—or was. *"Ich hat eine Kamaraden."*

Langer shook his head in the negative. "No, Teacher. I want Stefan on the radio. He'll work as the loader until he's broken in. Looks like he has good hands on him and at his age, he's probably quick and that's important."

"Come here, boy. Your name?"

"Manfried Ertl, *Herr Feldwebel*." He did everything but click heels.

"All right, Manny. You're one of us now and how much you pay attention and how quick you learn will determine how long you live. While you're with us, you will be one of us and this piece of tin will be your home. Take care of it. The *Feldwebel* crap you can forget. Just do as you are told and do it quickly."

Simultaneously, a thousand heads cocked themselves to the east listening. "*Jabos!* Hit the dirt!"

Like magic, men sought every piece of low ground and cover they could find. Carl grabbed the boy's arm and jerked him away from the tank, screaming, "Get away from the tank. It's the first thing they go for." Throwing the boy behind some brush, he buried his face in the dry dust.

Gorges of earth erupted, followed by brain-rupturing explosions. Soviet fighter bombers had spotted the tanks below and were determined not to let them get into action. One after another, they burst in oily blasts of flame as fuel tanks were hit. Counterfire came from a Luftwaffe Ack-ack unit using quad-mounted MG-42 light machine guns that could fire 2,400 rounds a minute each, pouring a stream of death into the dodging and darting Ilyuhsins with the red stars and smiling pilots who sensed an easy kill on the tanks below. The sitting Panthers were defenseless against the attack. A leg in a camouflaged trouser landed next to Langer's face, the foot still moving from side to side at the ankle. It didn't know it was dead yet.

Screams mingled with the staccato machine-gun fire and roaring thumps of blasting bombs, accented by the heavier Pom Pom of 20 mm5s getting into action. Gus ran dodging and twisting, throwing himself to the side of Langer, his steel pot giving him the look of an oversized Russian beetle. "Welcome home. I hope you appreciate how much trouble we went to, to have this display of fireworks for you." Spitting out a mouthful of red dust, he absently eyed the detached leg. "Wonder what size boot that is. I got a hole big enough to stuff a field marshal through in mine." Taking the foot, he looked at the boot, puckered his mouth and then tossed it and the leg farther away. "Wrong foot."

CHAPTER TWO

The Soviets finished their bombing-and-strafing runs, red stars and white trim clearly visible in the clear air. Their flight leader gave one lazy victory roll over the burning tanks below and followed his squadron, content to have sent a proper Russian welcome to the Nazis below. Such was his self-content that he never noticed the dark specks diving on him from twenty thousand feet. His first indication of something wrong came when his instrument panel was blown up by a burst from the 30mm cannon in the nose of the Gustav (Messerschmitt fighter), leading the swarm of four ME-109s now pouncing on the Shtormoviks that had done such slaughter below on their comrades.

Captain Ilye Popel, winner of the Order of Suvaron II class, screamed as the interior of his cockpit filled with flames, licking at his face, burning his hands into black charred stubs as he tried to control the wild earthward spin of his plane. His screams stopped when he was forced to take another breath in order to continue. Instead of air, his lungs filled with smoke and fire; mercifully he was dead four seconds before his aircraft disintegrated into a cloud of smoke and fire as it plowed into the field of ripening sugar beets below. Three others of his group shared his fate before the next ten seconds passed. The tankers and Panzergrenadiers below cheered as the Luftwaffe at least paid off a few of the bastards.

Langer pulled himself up from the sheltering earth and kicked Gus in the ass with the boot toe.

"All right, hero, get up and let's see what damages have been done."

Calling for Teacher and the others to join them, they checked their Panther. Luckily, only a near miss had gone off by them and there was no major damage, only a couple of bogie wheels that would have to be replaced and, a section of tread. The rest of the day was spent burying the dead and gathering up the separate parts of those who had been blown into bits and burying all the pieces together. They had long since stopped trying to match parts up with the proper owners. . . .

It was 1 July. With nightfall, Langer, Gus and the others settled down into the comfortable bunker they had appropriated from the previous occupants, who were now some ten miles distant, and began their interminable game of cards with Gus cheating as usual, but doing it so badly he usually lost anyway, so the others never let on they knew what he was doing. At ten hundred hours, Langer told them it was time to call it quits. They would have to work their asses off the next few days to get the tank in shape and familiarize themselves with it. Their previous mode of transportation, the old reliable Mark IV, had long since gone to that great scrap heap in the sky. Surely there was a Nordic Valhalla for all the good German tanks that died for the Reich and the Führer. Langer took the first watch even though they were well behind the front. Too many times units had been caught with their pants down when Ivan would make one of the unexpected lunges and a group of T-34s would come raging on them in the dark. At close quarters, the 76 mms they mounted could even take out one of the new Tigers that Doctor Porsche, their inventor, was so proud of.

Propping himself on the commander's seat, Langer leaned half out of the hatch and checked the MG-34, which he had scrounged earlier and mounted. Dragging deep on the cigaret butt he held cupped in his hands, Langer studied the moon-lit countryside, now so quiet, broken only by the sounds of a man snoring or sentry cursing quietly as he stumbled in the dark.

"Soon." The feeling was there and Langer had learned to believe his intuitions. This would be a big one; all the earmarks were there.

The long lines of infantry men moving up into positions to their left, trains by the hundreds bringing in the new tanks, and replacement stockpiles of munitions and supplies being built up in the rear. Reaching into the pocket of his camouflaged jacket, he took out a small bottle of white tablets, shook two out and popped them. . . . Benzedrine. One of the marvels of modern pharmaceutical developments. Soon, soon. They would be back in it. Ivan had gotten a lot smarter in the last year and a lot tougher. One thing was certain, hell waited out there in the dark.

The sleeping forms of his crew were only blacker masses in the darkness. Each had found a spot that suited him and curled up for the night wrapped in blankets like cocoons, the soft sounds of their shifting in their sleep were familiar; each had his own sounds. Teacher breathed through his mouth with small rasping gurgling noises and Gus, the walking bear, mumbled constantly in his dreams about booze, money or cunt. They were spaced out around their tank far enough from each other that if a lucky round from a Russian gun fell on them, they wouldn't all be taken out. Practical, professional men, they knew their business—which was death—the giving and the taking.

To the rear, working by the light of an oil lamp, Field Marshal Eric von Manstein poured over his charts and reports. Was anything omitted? Had all precautions been taken? His aristocratic face was a study in the best of the Prussian aristocracy.

It was all there, on the maps—pencil marks and lines that would spell victory or disaster. This was the trump card. Here they must win. All the reserves that Germany could scrounge were being thrown in. There was little left in the Fatherland to draw upon and what he had now, though the numbers were right, was not so good as the material he started out with on Operation Barbarossa two years ago.

They crossed the Russian frontier and raced to the gates of Moscow. Would it be enough? 900,000 men, 10,000 pieces of artillery and heavy mortars, 3,700 tanks and assault guns along with the Luftwaffe's contribution of 2,500 aircraft. This was it. In his heart he knew that if they failed here, the war could well be lost. There was no way to replace the men and materials. Italy had been stripped even though the Allied invasion of Sicily was imminent. He mused over what the British and Americans would run into if they had to face his army on the beaches along with the defenses that were already there. . . .

One hundred miles away, Marshal Zhukov was covering the same ground with General Rokossovsky, commander of Army Central. . . . Comrade Ivanov (Stalin) ordered there must be no failure.

"We have committed everything to this battle. We are thankful the Fascist pigs do not know our man in Switzerland who has kept us so well informed on their Operation Citadel. For months now, we have made every effort to prepare the greatest trap in the history of warfare. It will make Stalingrad look like child's play."

Pointing to the charts on the field table, Zhukov, with his peasant's face so much in contrast to the fine features of his German counterpart, ordered

Rokossovsky to go over his preparations—1,337,000 men, 20,000 pieces of artillery, rocket launchers and heavy mortars, 3,306 tanks and assault guns, 2,650 aircraft.

On the central front alone they had 5,100 mines per mile of front already laid and every day there would be more. Three thousand miles of trenches and antitank ditches were dug, their defenses were in six belts, one behind the other. Each would become successively stronger if the belt in front was forced to withdraw. They would then add their strength to the belt behind them and so forth until they bled the enemy dry. Zhukov gave one of his rare smiles, showing strong yellow teeth.

"It is enough. July 5—they will come and we are ready."

Teacher shook the others awake. Grumbling, they rolled out of their blankets, each in his own manner. Some had to take a leak, others needed a smoke to wake up. Langer sent Gus over to the mobile kitchen to get their morning rations. He had a knack for scrounging that was second to none, especially when he scared the shit out of the cooks by playing with a live grenade while he waited in a line that rapidly diminished when they saw him take the pin out and then reinsert it again and again, almost dropping the damned thing more than once. Gus did indeed have a way about him. For fun, he would set a concussion grenade on top of his steel helmet and stand there while it exploded. Knowing, as the old timers did, that explosives follow the line of least resistance and ninety-eight percent of the blast effect went straight up from the steel helmet, the worst he got was a ringing in the ears.

The next three days were spent in frantic preparations. Through intermittent rains, they familiarized themselves with their new home on tracks and its idiosyncrasies, painting the tank an off yellow and green camouflage pattern that would blend in well with the surrounding countryside. Extra tracks were placed on the turret sides and the ammo holders filled to capacity with extra 75 mms stacked by the driver along with their personal weapons, ready in case they had to unass the Panther in a hurry.

The steel leviathan weighed in at forty-five and one-half tons with a range of 110 road miles or half that cross country. It carried a long 75 with 79 rounds of ammo and 4,500 rounds of machine-gun ammo for the two MG-34s. Gus fell in love with the engine, a Maybach HL 230 twelve-cylinder diesel with 700 hp.

"This fucker's a beauty!" he cried out joyfully, slapping the side of the tank.

"At last we have something we can chew those damned T-34s up with. This little toy could take Moscow all by itself."

The night of the fourth they moved to their jump-off positions while a flight of Ju-88s and ME-109s buzzed the front in order to cover the track and engine noises. Quickly they camouflaged their tanks with brush and netting, waiting for the dawn while their officers received their battle orders and made last-minute changes. Midnight passed. It was 5 July, and the nearest thing to Armageddon the world had ever known was about to be born. . . .

First light broke hot and clear, a portent of the hell to come. The Soviet 17th Air Army was already crossing the lines separating the protagonists, heading to make a preemptive strike on the German air bases to the rear and destroy the bulk of the Luftwaffe aircraft while still on the ground, but the gods of war smiled on the Germans and one in particular screwed up the Russian plan.

FREYA, the name for the radar units stationed at the German airfields, picked up the incoming Soviets in time to alert their fighters. From General Siedeman's headquarters, the order went out to forget the planned scheduling and take off immediately. Scramble now and get everything that could fly in the air and off the vulnerable fields. Fighter engines screamed, their special whines like German eagles, airborne, climbing high to get above the confident Soviet squadrons who thought they were approaching sleeping bases. The Russian bombers were flying at 10,000 feet as the first wave of German fighters fell on them like hunting falcons from the heights, striking through the formations and breaking them up in panic, sending plane after plane crashing in flames to the earth. The MIG and Yak fighters did their best to protect their lumbering bigger brothers, but the altitude of the bombers left them at a disadvantage in dealing with the Fw-190s and ME-109s that raced around them, blasting them from the sky. In the first hour, the Soviets lost 120 aircraft and their even more pre-

25

cious crews as hundreds of German fighters hurled themselves with reckless abandon at everything that wore a red star. Before the day was over, another 300 would be added to the tally of Soviet losses, first blood to the Iron Cross.

Freya, the Nordic goddess of love and beauty, who also claimed half of those who fell on the field of battle for her own, served her people well this day.

The battle of Kursk was on; from all fronts came the order to attack. As volleys of artillery and mortar fire laid down barrages that made the earth erupt, trying to blast open a path for the armored beasts to race through.

CHAPTER THREE

Into the maelstrom of smoke, dust and flames, the tanks rumbled, engines straining, following the lines prepared by the engineers that night when they crept in to clear paths through the mine fields. The monstrous symphony of modern warfare had begun with an overture to death.

Gus laughed as he gunned the engine and ground a slit trench full of Russians into pulp. Locking one tread, the Panther pivoted, grinding the men beneath the threads into the dirt. A Tiger tank to the left exploded in a gout of black oily smoke as it hit an antitank mine. The sappers had missed this one. The crew bailed out of the hatches, only to be cut down by machine-gun fire, the Panzer grenadiers following in their wake, spread out, several falling to their faces as Ivan fought back with the tenacity of the Russian bear.

Teacher called for targets and Langer swung the

turret, checking the ring dial on the traverse indicator which showed him the relationship of the turret to the hull, bunker four hundred meters, load with HE. Teacher sighted. "Got it."

The recoil of the 75 rocked the Panther back on its suspension system. The front of the Soviet bunker erupted and several Russians ran from the back entrance followed by the stitching tracks of the MG-34 hull gun. The tracks overran two of the Russians and walked back and forth over their bodies. Even from this distance the dust puffing up from their uniforms where the bullets struck was easily visible. A gap in the Russian lines was made and the Panthers and Tigers of the 47th Panzer Corps poured through, followed by the grenadiers of the Gross Deutschland Division.

Langer's unit raced on, leaving the mopping up and taking of prisoners to the infantry. They had to advance regardless of risk. Their objective— Oboyan. In one swift rush, despite the Soviet's preparation, the main defensive line was torn open and General Krishoven's mechanized corps thrown into panic as the Tigers and Panthers flanked them, firing accurate controlled shots into the sides and turrets of the T-34s and self-propelled assault guns.

The 6th Guards Army, holding the perimeters facing the Germans, began to crumble with the loss of their armor and they knew there was nothing to stop the Fascists from overrunning them. They began to withdraw, trying to get back to the next defensive ring, only to be caught in the open by German artillery, which tore them to pieces and started the panic of a disorganized retreat. They dropped their guns and ran, every man for himself. Tanks raced after them, crushing them under the treads—they weren't worth wasting bullets on.

Gus screamed in glee as Teacher took a T-34 with a single shot that blew the turret of the enemy tank in the air and left the body of the tank's commander hanging from it half in, half out as the turret landed upside down on him. Another Panther was hit and Langer pulled his alongside to give the crew cover until they could get to a trench. All he had time to see was one of the tankers smash the brains out of a Russian with a shovel, and then the radio crackled in his ears with orders from the command tank. "On, on. Don't stop for anything again. Go, go, they're breaking."

Stefan began to hose the mustard-yellow uniforms in front of him, firing in short calculated bursts. He didn't want to burn up the machine gun. Coolly and carefully, Teacher sighted on a staff car and with a nod sent a screaming round into it, leaving only a smoking, burning frame. There was no trace of the Russians, they had just been atomized. To the right of them, the Panthers of GD were in trouble with a mine field and were stalled until the way could be cleared or another way out found.

The surviving Russians ran breathlessly, eyes wide with fear, trying to reach Syrtsevo on the Pena River, the last stronghold before Oboyan.

General Krivoshen hid in a gully, trying to assimilate what he could from a survivor of the 75th Motorized Battalion. He learned all were dead or taken prisoner and were already being hustled back to the holding pens in the rear of the German lines.

Krishoven leaped from the gully and climbed on top of an armored car in time to see his own staff car disappear from the blast. Kicking the driver in the back of the head, he screamed for him to get out of the way and take the machine down a ravine, heading away from the killer tanks. He would organize a counterattack from Srytsevo.

Langer's tank rumbled through the side of a peasant's hut, then stopped dead in its tracks inside the shack. Leaning down, Langer cursed Gus. "What the fuck are you doing, you moron? Get us out of here!"

Gus grinned. "Don't get your ass in an uproar, Sarge." Showing one gold tooth, he swung open his escape hatch and jumped out, taking two giant steps to a table surprisingly still standing in the wreckage. Grabbing an item from it, he leaped back through the hatch and into his seat. Battening the steel cover down over him, he gunned the motor and the forty-five tons of steel broke through the other side of the shack and back into the open. Teacher kicked Gus on the shoulder. "What the hell was that all about, you maniac?"

Reaching in his coat, Gus took out a bottle of vodka. "It might have gotten broken. . . ."

Teacher gave him a solid boot in the back. "You mean you stopped the whole fucking war for a bottle of vodka?"

Wounded, Gus said in hurt tones, "Well, if that's the way you feel about it, you don't have to drink any."

Teacher shook his head wonderingly and yelled up to Langer. "He stopped for a bottle of vodka."

Langer laughed. "What else? That dumb shit thinks that's the reason Hitler started this war—just for the vodka. He says it doesn't make sense to come to Russia for any other reason, so that's got to be it. Maybe he knows something we don't."

The smell of diesel fumes and cordite left a sour taste in the mouth. SPAAAAANG. A Russian round bounced off the glacis shield in front and bounced off to explode elsewhere.

"Where is he?" Langer swung the turret using the periscope.

"Got him. Over by that field of trees. The bastard's dug in; just the turret showing. Looks like a KV-I. Can you take him, Teacher?"

The scholar sighted and corrected his azimuth readings a little.

"Fire." The shell burst directly in front of the Russian tank. Teacher spat on the floor. Before Langer could say anything, he resighted, saying, "Don't get in a sweat. After all, I'm not used to this thing yet. Give me a little time."

The next round took the KV-I right at the junction of the hull and turret, exploding the tank from the inside and turning the gunner and loader into shriveled cinders.

A sense of urgency and panic drove them on. One by one, more of the group were knocked out by the Soviet Pakfronts, copied and improved from the German model. The use of up to ten antitank guns under one commander could bring tremendous fire-power to bear on a single tank. The first indication you were facing one was usually when your neighbor blew up. That, and the technical problems with the new Panthers, gave Langer a lonesome feeling, as the crackle in his radio informed him he was alone with no infantry support. Upon realization of this, Gus locked the right tread and cut ass back to the rear about four miles, where he pulled into a ravine shared by a couple of Wespe self-propelled guns. The sight of their 105s gave them a feeling of security. Infantry from the GD were digging in for the night.

Had it been that long? They had made six miles. A flight of Shtormoviks droned overhead, the Mikulin engines humming as the pilot and rear gunner looked for targets on the ground.

Brush and branches were quickly thrown on top of the Panther to conceal her from the eyes above. Soon darkness would cover them. Haumpmann Heidemann called asking for his position. The remainder of the unit was digging in for the night with a bunch of Tiger Is of the 6th Company, 1st SS Panzer regiment commanded by Rudolf von Ribbentrop, son of the Reich's famed foreign minister. The crackle of Maxims on the Soviet side let them know Ivan was still there. Angling their tank into position where only the turret showed above the edge of the gully, they waited for the night. Ivan would come. He couldn't afford not to. The night was the time when their numbers gave them the greatest advantage.

The Guards regiment they had mauled would

even now be creeping out, grouping together in small knots of men, listening to the haranguing of the Komissars whipping them into a fighting fervor to destroy the Fascist beasts who dared step on the soil of the mother Russia by the dozens and then the hundreds. These small pockets emerged, then began to join together, forming larger ones; thousands of Russians had been bypassed in the tank fight and now they would have to face them in the dark.

Langer left Teacher in the turret with the binoculars and sent Gus off to scrounge some chow from the grenadiers. They had plenty on board, but if there was food to be had, they would save theirs. Young Ertl kept close to Langer, his lips still trembling from controlled fear, his face pale. Grunting, Carl lit a butt and stuck it between the boy's lips.

"Take a drag. It will help. You did good today. Now find a place close to Gus when he gets back and stay with him. That ugly old bear may not be fit for the drawing rooms of Europe, but out here, he has a knack for surviving. Maybe some of it will rub off on you."

Langer found the officer in charge of the grenadiers and lunched down beside him. The major was going over his charts, marking their position and noting where the other units of the assault force were digging in for the night. Darkness was closing in and in the distance, long columns of smoke from burning tanks showed the Luftwaffe was still at work. From the north came the long distant rumble of artillery barrages being laid.

Turning to Langer, the major—his face dirty and

33

uniform less than picture-book perfect—squinted at him through grime-laden lids.

"You the one with the Mark V?"

Carl nodded.

"Good. We will need you before this night is done. The bastards knew we were going to hit them today. They knew when and where. I'm Kruger, major by the grace of our Führer in this glorious social experiment. Fuck it. Where's your beast at?"

Langer pointed down the ravine to the Panther.

"Good enough. Leave it there. I'll send over a squad to give you cover for the night. After it gets dark, pull it back a little from the edge of the gully and face it down the ravine so you can use your hull MG. The turret gun will still be able to fire over the lip of the gully."

Carl nodded agreement. The man knew his business.

Lighting up a smoke for himself, he drew it deep into his lungs, holding a moment and then exhaling through his nostrils.

"Where are we, Major? I can just get radio contact with my company leader but we've been weaving in and out of those damned antitank ditches for hours."

Pointing a dirty fingernail, Kruger indicated a point on the map. "Here. Just north of Butovo." He looked at the shoulder tabs of the Panzer man. "You're with the 26th Pz, right?" Then, not waiting for an answer, "They're on the right flank about four kilometers behind and we are, my good friend and ally, the leading element of this action."

A whining hum followed by the crack of a rifle

shot made them slap the sides of the gully automatically. Langer spit the mangled butt out of his mouth where he had snuffed it out by pushing his face into the ground. Taking a bit of tobacco off his tongue with a dirty hand he said, "Sounds like a Tokarev. Probably a sniper with a scope. Do you have anyone here to take him out?"

Kruger shook his head. "No, but I'll send a couple of boys out to get him when it gets dark. He's been taking pot shots for the last hour; hasn't hit anyone but it can ruin a man's digestion when he gets too close."

Two *Sanitätsmen* carrying a stretcher with a wounded stabsfeldwebel on it passed, bent low. The man on the stretcher moaned, his hands holding his stomach. A battle dressing covered a hole in his gut.

Kruger shook his head. "A good man. Shrapnel from a T-34 burst. . . ." Langer looked closely at the wounded man's face as he passed. He had seen the look too many times before, that distant expression that even pain could not hide. A certain look to the eyes that meant he was dying.

"He's a goner."

Kruger nodded agreement. "All right, Sergeant, enough of this bullshit. Get back to your people and take care of them. If I can do anything for you, let me know." Kruger turned his back and moved off down the gully, talking to a man here and there, giving a pat on the back or kick in the ass as was needed.

Approvingly Langer watched him. Good man. A spinning ricochet said their sniper was still out there

—trying his best but to little avail.

Gus joined him on the way back to the Panther, carrying five loaves of bread and an armful of ersatz sausage which everyone swore was made from the cadavers of diseased hyenas. Only Gus seemed to like them, but then he liked everything. He was a walking septic tank. Langer watched in amazement as a long link of sausages disappeared into the gaping orifice that served as a mouth for Gus. "A walking septic tank, that's what he is."

CHAPTER FOUR

Ilye Shimilov scanned the German positions through an artillery periscope. Holding the rank of captain, he still had the final authority over the commander of the guards battalion that would attack this night. He had proved his fitness time and again, and more than once he had personally shot laggards or those who failed to show the proper revolutionary spirit in the back of the neck with his Nagant revolver. He preferred it over the newer automatic Tokarev pistols. Revolvers were old-fashioned, but they seldom jammed. He was satisfied with what he saw. From the outposts he had received the strength and disposition of the Germans facing him.

Two self-propelled guns and a single Panther, all told about eighty men in the gully which sat on a small rise. He had at his disposal seven T-34s and two KV-Is. That and the assault battalion of the

199th Guards would be more than enough to wipe out this small pocket of Fascists.

There was about a half-hour of light left. Langer put his rations in the turret and strapped on a couple of extra pouches of magazines for the MP-40 submachine gun he took out of the tank. Stuffing his long Kar-98 bayonet into his belt, he tapped Teacher on the shoulder and said, "I'm going out for a look see." One thing he had learned over the years was to get a look at his position from the enemy's point of view, to see where the most likely spot was for them to come from and check for low points in which troops could mass unseen.

Teacher nodded. "Be careful, my friend. We need you here. Don't let Ivan talk you into going to one of the rest camps beyond the Urals."

Carl smiled, put a couple of egg grenades into his jacket pocket and slipped over the top of the gully and into the brush. His splinter camouflage blended well into the bushes. He crawled slowly and easily, instinctively staying in the lowest ground possible. No dip was too small not to serve as he worked his way out, crawling until his knees and elbows felt as if they were working their way through the canvaslike fabric of his jacket and trousers. Going out about three hundred meters, he hunched in a shell hole with the remains of an unidentifiable corpse. Not even a shred of uniform was left to show if he was German or Russian. Taking out his notebook, he quickly drew a sketch of the German positions from this viewpoint, making special notes of the small dips in which Ivan could rush them from no more than fifty meters. That distance in the dark could be covered in seconds.

Crawling on, he heard a rustle in the high grass to his left. He froze. The sky was getting dark and shadows were long on the ground. Straining, he waited. Another rustling of bushes. Whoever it was, was near and coming his way. Slowly he took the bayonet out of his belt and held it near his face.

Squirming slightly to face the sounds, he tensed, gathering his legs under him, ready to leap or run if there were too many. A shadow showed itself lengthwise to him between some brush and a patch of high grass. Drawing a long slow breath, he held it in a moment and then lunged, belly low to the ground, his blade ready to strike into the body of the intruder.

The intruder turned just in time for Langer to see his face. He turned his blade away but still landed on the man with a thump.

Major Kruger heaved a sigh of relief. "What the hell are you doing out here?"

"The same thing you are, I imagine." He noted the small hand-drawn map in the major's hand.

Somewhat testily Kruger reprimanded Langer. "Next time, Sergeant, if it wouldn't be too much trouble, would you kindly inform me of your plans before you cut my throat. And put that damned ugly blade away. It gives me the chills just thinking how close you came."

The two conferred for a moment on what they had seen and made their way back separately to the ravine. Slithering on his belly, Langer slid down to the bottom as his crew gathered around.

Gus was still stuffing food into his mouth between swallows of vodka, making the most atrocious feeding sounds he had ever heard, gulping, choking, grunting and farting—all at the same time. Unbelievable.

"Where's those grenadiers the major said we could have?"

Teacher gave a low whistle and an *Obergefreiter* joined them from the shadows. He was a dark wiry man, his belt stuffed with stick grenades and an MP on his chest. "Koch, Wather. I guess we're to work together tonight."

Langer nodded. "Good enough. What do you have with you?"

Koch pointed to the shadows in niches of the gully. "Seeing as how you're on the far end of this ditch, the major sent me with two MG-34s and ten riflemen. Where do you want us?"

Moving to the side of the tank, Teacher handed them a flashlight; covering the glow, they went over the small notebook map Carl had made.

"From out there, I could see two approaches they could take, one just to our left is low enough for infantry to get close enough without being seen; the other is a trench farther out. They could get to us from that and come down the ravine. We'll take care of the tank ourselves. I want you to place half your men and one MG on the ridge. Put the others and your remaining MG about forty meters down the gully from us. Place them on the far side. That way, if Ivan comes down, you let them get past you and we'll have them between your MG and the Panther's hull gun. I'll give you one minute after the first firing starts to get your men out of the way.

You come back to us on the far side of the ridge and join us here. At that time, we'll cut loose with the seventy-five to finish off whatever's left of the Ivans in the gully."

Koch nodded agreement. "Very good. I like it. They won't expect anyone to be on the far side of the gully. Should work out pretty good. Make sure you give me that minute before you cut loose with that cannon."

Splitting his men up, he gave them their instructions and took the rest down the gully with him, disappearing into the shadows of the last light.

Crackling in the distance, a Russian light machine gun answered by the rapid chatter of a German MG-42. . . .

General Oberst Hoth received the day's after action reports with a sense of forboding. Reviewing the positions of his troops, uneasiness worried at the edge of his mind. Too slow. They had not reached their objectives. Ivan was ready for them. True, they had made five miles of penetration over all, but that did not mean that the Soviet lines were penetrated—not the way they had prepared their system of ring defenses. The day had started off badly enough when Lauchert's brigade of Panthers had stalled in an undetected mine field. It took hours for the pioneers to clear a lane. All the time, Russian artillery was having a field day on the immobilized tanks. The rains of the past days had served to turn the low ground near Beresvyy into a bog where one tank after another came to a standstill with mud up to the skirts and covering the treads. The only success was the capture of Cherkakoye, where the flame throwers mounted on the Mark IIIs had used their flaming hoses to good effect in burning out the houses and bunkers. The hissing jets of fire had a range of almost eighty meters and turned the inside of the Soviet bunkers into flaming ovens designed for the cooking of human flesh.

Turning off the lamp he sat on the edge of his field cot in the dark, thinking about tomorrow. The Knight's Cross glistened in the reflected light of a distant Russian flare, lighting up the night sky and then fading into a cinder and becoming one with the darkness again.

Langer watched the flare wink out. It was over to his left where the SS men were dug in. Teacher lit his pipe, shielding the bowl with his hand. Motioning for Teacher to take his place on the turret machine gun, he clambered down and went to where Koch's infantrymen were on the ridge. Moving alongside the machine gunner, he squinted into the dark.

"Anything happening?"

A negative shake of the head was answer enough. Taking his binoculars, he focused them and slowly searched the dark. They're out there, I know it. A short muffled cry and then silence came to him out of the dark to the front.

The gunner spoke quietly. "The major said he'd take out that sniper. For my money, he should have left him alone. That blind bastard couldn't hit anything. Now they might send up one who knows how to shoot. But the major's always had a hard-on for snipers, ever since one shot his left ball off outside Stalingrad."

Langer chuckled. "Left ball, huh? How can you be sure he can get a hard-on for anything?" The gunner smiled in the dark . . . good question.

Snick. The sound of a rifle bolt closing.

"Somewhere out there. Hard to tell how far. Sound is different at night; could be twenty meters or a hundred."

The gunner nodded. "I heard. Bet they're in the small piece of low ground to the left. He shifted his gun over to where it touched one of the stakes he had driven into the ground on each side of his weapon. They served as markers for him in the dark.

"There's another one. They're getting ready. What say we shake them up a little."

Langer thought about it for a moment. "No. We better let them make the first move. I don't want to give your gun position away too soon. We'll wait awhile. They won't be long now. I'm going back to the tank and when you're sure they are out in the open, give a whistle and I'll light them up for you."

The gunner grinned again. "*Zum befehl, Herr Feldwebel* (at your command)."

"You've got HE in the tube, don't you, Teacher?" The esthetic-looking scholar confirmed that they had high-explosive rounds ready and to hand.

"Good, infantry will come first. We'll have time to load for tanks when we hear them coming. I think they're going to try and surprise us first without any mortar fire or artillery preparation. They lay that on us if they can't infiltrate."

Gus sat on the go position, ready to turn on his engine and start up. Stefan was on the hull gun waiting. Humming to himself, Manny stood ready to load whatever shell was required and Teacher entertained himself by quoting passages from Schiller to himself. Langer took the flare pistol and loaded it. A short soft whistle. Carl motioned Teacher to get on his gun while he took the MG on the turret. Raising the flare pistol, he fired a long burning arc that raced overhead like a sky rocket, leaving a trail of sparks behind it to burst into a searing flash of white light. Beneath the glow the Russians stood frozen in their tracks by the unexpected illumination.

"Fire!" Langer's MG joined that of the gunner on the ridge in sending rapid bursts of fire into the massed bodies of the Russians. The chatter of the MG's was joined by the slower cranking of the Mauser rifles of the infantrymen.

Ilye Shimilov screamed orders and the guardsmen hurled themselves at the German positions shouting "*Urra Stalino.*" The rest of the trench opened up and withering fire erupted from all guns, hosing the Russians down into dark masses of dead and dying. And still they came on with the high-speed, rapid chatter of the burp guns competing with that of the Schmeissers. And men died.

The gunners on the ridge held the Russian attack.

Ilye Shimilov screamed in frustration and shot two guardsmen in the back of the head in order to provide the others with the proper spirit. He was going to shoot a third when a bullet from a Mauser smashed into his forehead and blew most of his brains out, leaving a gaping hole you could stick a fist in. The rifleman who hit him laughed as he told his neighbor, "I told you, cut the noses off and you will blow the shit out of anything you hit. Dumdums ought to regular issue."

His dialogue ended when a grenade blew his face off and left him gurgling wetly in the bottom of the gully. The Russians to the front faded back into the dark, firing as they went. A ricochet bouncing off the turret told Langer that they were coming from the ravine now. Swinging his MG around, he waited a second and the rapid, distinct sound of Koch's MG-34 told him it was time to let go with his own. He swept the gully in front of him from side to side, his weapon joined by Stefan's in the hull. Counting slowly, he gave Koch his minute and ordered Teacher to fire the 75 mm set to the lowest position. The shells burst in the middle of a packed group of about sixty Russians, sending arms, legs and torsos into different directions. Teacher fired as fast as he could be reloaded.

The rest of the trench was involved with their own troubles and had no one to spare for them. Each had to hold his own or die. The grenadiers on the edge of the ravine turned their weapons to point down the gully and began firing and throwing grenades as fast as the pins could be pulled. Koch's group stayed on their side of the ravine to keep out of the way of the Panther's gun and continued to send a hail of fire into the Russians below. The exploding shells of the Panther tore the attackers to pieces.

A cry from the side of the ravine jerked Langer's head around.

"Enemy tanks. They're coming. I can hear them."

A runner from Major Kruger raced up to them. Breathless, he climbed up to Carl. "The old man says you are to pull back up to the other side of the ditch and cover us while the Wespes get to some high ground."

Langer acknowledged the order and told Gus to start her up. The Maybach roared into life and the Panther moved off. Langer kept the turret facing the Russians and Teacher continued to fire, giving cover while the infantry withdrew. Flares started to pop overhead, lighting up the whole area in blinding brilliance. The artillery to the rear was giving what support they could in response to Kruger's frantic plea for support. The flares showed a wedge of T-34s led by two KV-Is moving across the field, all guns firing.

Langer's tank moved up the opposite rim of the ridge. Without waiting to be told, Teacher reloaded with a piercing scream and sighted on the approaching tanks. Taking the leader in his sight, he nodded for the okay and fired, the round knocking the tread off, leaving the T-34 turning in circles, a wounded beast waiting for the death blow which was not long in coming. The crew burned inside as the fuel tanks went up and then exploded when the flames reached the stacks of shells inside, blowing the tank completely over.

The Wespes had reached ground suitable for the use of their powerful 105s. The assault guns had a limited traverse but were in their element in anti-tank fighting from prepared positions. One after another, Russian tanks were knocked out until the field in front no longer needed the flares of the artillery to light it up. The burning hulks of Soviet armor provided all the light they needed. As soon as the tanks were done in, the Wespes shifted over to antipersonnel rounds, firing shells that exploded above the heads of the panic-stricken Russians, smashing them into the earth while the combined machine-gun and rifle fire of the grenadiers of the Gross Deutschlanders stitched them back and forth, the tracers from the MGs like racing fireflies. They sought out the soft bodies of the attackers. The Russians broke and disappeared back into the dark, leaving their wounded behind. They had enough. Only one KV-I returned. Eight lay burning on the field. They never got closer than two hundred meters to the gully.

CHAPTER FIVE

Immediately after the Russians withdrew, Major Kruger ordered all the men back into the gully, including the Wespes and Langer's Panther. Carl thought he was crazy when he ordered all guns to fire at nothing from the trench for a full five minutes and then ordered them back out to take up positions a thousand meters to the rear.

It wasn't until Ivan began to lay artillery and heavy mortars on the position they had just left that he understood why. By going back to the gully and firing they let Ivan think they were still there and let them shell empty positions all night while they rested in peace further back. Once the new defensive perimeters were set and the sentries stationed, the rest could settle down for a few hours of badly needed sleep. They had been lucky this night. If Ivan hadn't tried to get so cute and creep up on them without any artillery or mortar fire beforehand, it might well have been a different story. As it was they had only nine dead and seven wounded, two critically, and these were laid by the Wespes and were being cared for by their medics.

Langer and Teacher took the first watch. Teacher filled his ever-present pipe and sucked in deep on the aromatic smoke while Langer lit up another Juno.

"A long day, right, Teacher?"

"It could have been longer or shorter. It's all a matter of perspective."

Carl stripped to the waist and rinsed himself with a careful measure from his canteen, wiping away the surface grime and powder. The water, even though lukewarm, felt cool on his skin. Teacher looked at the mass of scars on his tank leader's torso. Some were thin lines like threads of white; others were deep gouges that puckered at the edges and one on his left wrist that ran all the way around. . . .

"I don't guess you're ever going to tell me how you got so chopped up, so I guess I'll just have to ask. If you don't want to talk, it's all right." He took a couple of short puffs to keep the pipe lit.

"It's all right, Teacher. The old scars came from when I was a kid and in a car wreck; I went through the windshield and got cut up pretty good. The others came from an assortment of accidents—some from a train wreck in Switzerland in 1934 and the others from jealous husbands; they look worse than they are."

Teacher moved to where he could see Carl's chest and pointed to a long deep scar right in the center of the chest. "What about that one! I know that had to be serious."

Langer touched the scar. "Well, let's just say that's one I don't want to talk about."

Teacher nodded. "As you wish. Now tell me, how are things at home? What news? We really haven't had a chance to talk since you got back from the training regiment."

Letting the air dry him, he sat down next to Teacher on the turret. "Not good. The Americans and British are bombing night and day and all but the essentials are gone, though the black market is active enough, if you have money—or something to trade. But what bothers me the most are the rumors and stories of what's going on at places where civilians are kept in camps. A couple of names that have cropped up are Auschwitz and Buchenwald. I don't know, Teacher, I have seen trainloads of Jews being sent back from Poland and Russia, whole families in cattle cars. I asked an SD man about it at one of the stations and he said they were going to relocation centers . . . but I just don't know. The things I have heard are not good."

Teacher nodded slowly. "I know what you are talking about. I have heard them too. It's the SS, the bully boys of the Totenkopf, the Jew baiters and toughs from the streets of the thirties." Teacher spat on the side of the tank, missing his mark on the ground.

"Bastards."

"Here at the front we don't get any of that shit or hear much of it, but recently they have been sending some of those black-uniformed heroes to the front to fill out the ranks of the Waffen SS and with them, they bring their sickness."

Langer shook his head, the thin hairline scar giving him a bitter look that came out in his words, "I don't know if we deserve to win if the stories are true, Teacher. I don't know if we're going to win anyway. Russia is just too big, and for every tank that's turned out in the factories in Germany, the Russians turn out twenty. They can afford the losses. If we don't win soon, I don't think we ever will, and if the stories are right, I don't want us to. Look, we have all shot some prisoners when it was necessary, when we couldn't take them with us and couldn't send them back or let them go. That's one thing. But the horrors I have heard are too much and believe me, Teacher, I have been around more than you might believe."

Teacher thumped his pipe out in the cup of his hand, dropping the ashes. "You can talk to me like that, but be careful what you say around anyone else. You know the punishment for spreading sedition and defeatest talk."

"Well, it's time to wake Gus and the youngster up. We can still get a couple of hours sack before morning."

Gus and Manny took their places on the turret while Teacher and Langer rolled up in their blankets. Like all soldiers they knew how to sleep instantly—one deep breath, close the eyes and out.

Gus spent the hours until dawn regaling Manny with stories of his amorous adventures while working as a whorehouse bouncer in Stuttgart. Manfried learned more that night about female anatomy than he could have in twenty years of normal living, but then whoever said Gus was "normal." Everything he did was oversized and exaggerated; he ate more, talked more, drank more and lied more than anyone in the army and that included the general staff and Herr Schiklegruber, as he referred to the SS's holy German, the Austrian Führer.

Manny was aghast at the disrespect shown the leader. Never had he heard anyone say anything detrimental about him before. It was unheard of, but he couldn't help laughing when Gus told him that Hitler would have never made it, if he had kept his real name. After all, it would nearly be impossible to imagine 20,000 black-dressed SS men at a party day rally in Nuremberg shouting "Heil Schiklegruber." No indeed, there was a lot to a name.

By the time of the first false light of predawn creeping over the fields, he was certain he was sitting next to either a madman or superman—possibly both. Scratching the stubble of beard, Gus stood up on the side of the tank and undid his pants and took a leak, his stomach rumbled and he leaped from the tank telling Manny to watch things and ran off to do some looting for breakfast. The four pounds of sausage was eaten before last night's attack. Gus was a man who needed to keep his strength up. After all, one never knew when he might run into some of the Russian female mortar crews. God. How he would like to have a week interrogating some of the large-titted, broad-hipped Russian female officers. He would teach them soon enough who the master race was; after all, did not a pecker bear a strong resemblance to the German helmet. And he, being the pride of the Panzer Corps, had the finest example of one available for miles.

Gus's logic escaped Manny, but then most of the things Gus said he missed. After Gus left, he self-consciously opened his trousers and took a good look at his own organ. Controlling a giggle, he thought: "You know, it does look like a German helmet, but doesn't everyone's look the same?" He'd have to ask Gus about that when he came back.

Langer awoke to the sound of engines starting up, which brought him to instant awareness. Gus was back with a helmet full of eggs and the hind-quarter of a hog. He was breaking the egg tops off and sucking them out as fast as he could, smacking his lips and making that awful gurgling sucking sound he had when he normally fed.

"Here," he said as he set the helmet full of eggs down. There were ten. "These are for you and the others. I already ate mine."

Grinning, Langer looked up, "And how many was that, Gus?"

"Only a dozen, more or less. I didn't want to make a pig of myself, you know. Have to watch my figure."

Stefan leaned out of the hatch. "You don't have to worry about making a pig of yourself, you're already a walking piece of suet. God already took care of that for you."

Nonplussed, Gus tossed him the hindquarter. "None of your lip, now, or Uncle Gus will spank.

Here, put our lunch away and out of sight before any of the GD boys see it. It was to be their lunch, but the chef still has one left to spread around."

The haunch quickly disappeared into the interior.

Major Kruger strode up to them, his eyes still red. "Well, fellows, you can come with us or try to get back to your unit on your own, though I think we'll end up in the same place eventually. At any rate, I just wanted to let you know you did good work last night and if you ever want a transfer, give me a call. We're moving out now. The rest of the division is moving up. General Hoerlein wants us to take the bridge over the Psel south of Oboyan today, so we better get cracking."

"Thanks for the offer, Major, but I think we better try and contact our own batallion first. Stefan, see if you can get the captain on the radio."

Captain Heidemann's voice crackled over the earphones. Langer reported the night's activities and then turned the set off.

"We're to rendezvous with the batallion by the railroad track going from Belgorod to Rzhavka. There's a burned-out KV-I on a hill that we can spot on. It's only about five miles, so let's warm her up and get going."

Hatches opened as he waved farewell to Kruger, and the Panther rumbled off up out of the gully, treads tearing up ground as they lurched and crested the lip and Gus swore as his head bounced and struck the edge of his open hatch. Crossing the field, the tank ground bodies underneath. As the

forty-five tons of steel approached another pile of
bodies, one suddenly got up and started sprinting
away.

Langer swung the MG-34 around and fired a
short burst in front of him: *"Stoi, Ruki verkh."*

The Russian froze in his tracks. Following orders,
he raised his hand high crying out: *"Nix Schiessen!
Tovarish, Nix Schiessen!"*

The man had no weapon, so Langer motioned for
him to come to the tank, which was sitting on idle.
"Idisodar charoscho. Come quickly."

The Ivan obeyed with alacrity. Carl motioned for
him to sit on the rear behind the turret, after making sure he had nothing that would go boom on
him. The Russian had the face of one who had been
born on the crossroads of Asia; bright dark eyes in a
weathered face, three gold teeth when he smiled.
Langer had to almost forcibly keep Gus at the controls when he saw the miniature gold mine in the
prisoner's mouth. He already had his pliers out,
ready to do a little digging. Sulking, he obeyed and
went back to driving the tank, cursing at how unfair
it was for a sergeant to interfere with free en-
terprise. The Russian kept close to Langer and
pointed down the hatch at Gus: *"Germanski,
Khrpikj djavol."*

Langer laughed. "You got that right, Ivan. He is
a crazy devil. Just keep your mouth shut around
him and maybe he'll forget, though I wouldn't bet
on it."

Spotting the burned out KV-I on the hill, they
swung past it and saw the rest of their batallion

loading up with petrol and ammo.

"Good. We're low on both. Find a place in the line."

Langer left the others to see to the servicing of the tank and took the Tatar with him to report to Captain Heidemann.

Heidemann was conferring with a dispatch rider on a motorcycle but waved him over. "Glad to see you back, Langer. What do you have here?" He pointed to the Russian.

"Hitchhiker."

Heidemann sighed, "Well, we don't have time for a prisoner. You found him, you take care of him."

The dark little man knew instinctively his life was being handed over to the man with the scarred face. "*Nix schiessen, spasibo Germanski, Yuri.*" Then pointing to himself, "*Nix Stalin.*" He made the rocking motion of a mother and child with his arms. Langer watched the little man and shook his head, smiling to show everything was all right.

"*Germanski, nix schiessen, Yuri.*" The little wiry man lit up, his gold teeth flashing. He knelt down and placed Langer's boot on the top of his head. "*Dosvedanya. Stalin kaputt.*"

Teacher came up while this was going on and Langer told what the captain said. "I guess we'll keep him for a while. You take him back and get him out of that Russian uniform or he won't make it through the day."

Teacher nodded. "You think it's wise to do that? We might wake up with our throats slit one morning. These devils are mighty handy with a blade."

"I think it's all right. I know something of the people, and the little scene you witnessed where he put my foot on his head made me his master. He's not a true Russian, he's from the steppes to the east. Just a poor bastard who's been caught up in this thing like the rest of us, but once a Tatar acknowledges someone as his master, he's faithful to the death."

Teacher still had a puzzled look on his face, but the tone which Langer used said he knew what he was talking about.

Taking Yuri by the arm, Carl guided him back to their tank, where the rest of the crew chipped in pieces of clothing to make him a semblance of a uniform. Before Teacher would let him change, he made him take a bath, a thing which seemed to wound the Tatar's dignity worse than being captured, but he complied after Gus took out his pliers. Murmuring '*Khrpikj djavol*" he kept a wary eye on Gus and his pliers while he washed.

Langer and the others received their orders for the day's mission and returned to their vehicles; getting them positioned, they waited for the order to move out. Yuri fairly sparkled at being able to ride on the tank in the new uniform. When the tanks rumbled and clanged their way forward, he cried happily so all could hear, "*Stalino kaputt. Urra Germanski.*"

CHAPTER SIX

The next eleven days were a nightmare of fire and death. Tanks stood at point-blank range firing into each other. The fastest crews survived. Anti-tank guns from both sides took a deadly toll. The German Nebelwerfers were answered by the rushing roar of the Stalin organ, the Katyushin multiple rocket launchers. The infantry fought with guns and grenades locked in the greatest struggle of history. By the thousands and tens of thousands they died. On the sector of the Gross Deutschland Division alone, three hundred German tanks were locked in a death grip with seven hundred Russian tanks like pit bulldogs; neither side would let go until dead. At night tanks would ram each other in the dark. There was no respite. Each knew the battle would foretell the future. Everything was staked on this card.

Yuri had become one with the crew, learning to

leap inside the turret escape hatch with amazing speed when the shit started. His sharp eyes had more than once spotted an enemy tank and given them the advantage of the first shot. Eleven days and they had only advanced five kilometers past Verkhopenye. The first battle for the prize of Kursk was ready. Both sides licked their wounds and prepared for the morning of the twelfth.

From Stavka the Russian high command had come, one of those Hitler-type commands that all soldiers fear. General Vatutin showed the order to his military council member, Nikita Khrushchev. The Germans must not break through to Oboyan. This order, like that Hitler had given to Paulus of the 6th Army at Stalingrad, meant stand or die. So be it.

On a hill overlooking Prokhorovka, General Romistrov gave the order for Soviet counterattack. Eight hundred and fifty armored beasts revved their engines and moved out, mostly T-34s, with a sprinkling of self-propelled guns. They advanced, their crews confident. They rumbled across the flats leading to the Prokhorovka just in time to meet the new assault of Hausser's SS Panzer Corps, six hundred Panther Mark IVs and nearly a hundred of the massive Tigers with their high-velocity 88s. They met in the orchard and fields. Soon each tank was on its own, whirling and firing. The sound of exploding armor merged into the continuous roar of cannon fire. Overhead the two air forces met, each trying to give their side the advantage. Shtormoviks raced low over the groves spewing death from their machine guns and rockets while the Stukas of Captain Rudel dived screaming to smash at the vulnerable rears of the T-34s. Rudel's tank killers, armed with the new 3.7-cm antitank cannons, blew tank after tank to pieces, turrets bursting from their housings to land yards away. Crashing fighters and bombers added their rubble to the fields below as they whirled and dived, twisting in a *danse macabre*. The sky darkened from the smoke of burning tanks and the smoke hung low over the fields, masking whole sections of the front until the only way to tell who your opponent was, was to smash into him close enough to see the faces of the commanders in their turrets frantically trying to kill you.

Crews able to escape their burning vehicles hid in the ditches and trenches trying to bury themselves in the earth. Most became part of it when the treads of an assaulting or retreating tank mashed them into jellied pulp. As often as not the tank was one of their own.

Langer's battalion was assaulting from the western flank and penetrated the Soviets from the side. The Panthers did deadly work as they raced into the confused mass of milling steel monsters until they too were lost in the maelstrom and each fought separate and alone. Burning Tigers littered the ground. The range at which they fought was so short that even the lesser guns of the T-34s ripped them apart.

Yuri, standing at the side of the Panther; hurled grenades at Russian crews hiding in shell holes while the rapid high-speed chatter of the machine guns swept everything in front of them.

Langer's Panther slid out of control down a gully, only to be stopped by smashing into a T-34 with a broken tread. Neither one could turn its cannon to fire on the other. Yuri screamed like a banshee and leapt on the turret of the Russian, beating at the closed hatch with egg grenades, uselessly. Gus frantically worked the controls trying to back away far enough for Teacher to put a round into Ivan but just dug them in deeper. Langer yelled for Manny to hand him up a shell and taking it, jumped from his turret to that of the Russians. He placed the round under the overhang at the rear of the turret and taking a grenade from Yuri, he set it by the shell and pulled the pin, throwing himself and Yuri off to land behind the Russian. The grenade set off the 75 mm and blew the turret clear from the T-34. Amazingly only the commander was killed in the explosion. The rest of the crew sat at their positions stunned, blood pouring from nostrils and ears. Yuri screamed with joy and threw himself into the interior slashing throats with the long-bladed butcher knife Langer had given him the previous day. He killed them all and rose from the hull dripping blood and smiling.

Holding a Russian's severed head in each hand by the hair and showing them proudly to Langer, he said, "Yuri good Germanski, *nyet?*"

Langer rose, still somewhat stunned from the explosion, and told Yuri to throw them back. They didn't have time for souvenirs. Disappointed, Yuri spat in each of the faces and tossed the heads back into the hull with the bodies they had come from. The Russian medics could match them up later.

Gus finally got enough distance from the T-34 to be able to pull back and get enough of a run to break out of the ditch his own treads had created. Lurching, the Panther clambered out of the gully as Langer and Yuri leaped back on and climbed inside in time to see a MIG smash into the earth and explode not seventy meters in front of them.

Overhead the killer—a Gustav ME-109—wheeled off after a twin-engine bomber. Time lost all meaning. Minutes became hours. Hours seemed like eternity. Everything was exaggerated—the sounds, colors, tastes. The smell of cordite and burning fuel oil clogged their nostrils. The battle was winding down. In an area of less than ten square miles, each side had lost over three hundred tanks. Romistrov ordered his survivors to withdraw, racing to the rear, the turrets still facing the Germans and firing. The survivors ran, leaving the field of slaughter to the Germans. As Langer followed in pursuit, his tank seemed to rise up into the air and then fall back. The crashing of his tank was covered by the explosion of the Russian shell that had blown the treads off. Smoke was coming from the engine. These damned Panthers had a tendency to burn all too easily. Gus swore like a madman as he bailed out of his escape hatch. The others joined to take cover in a shell hole, taking their personal weapons with them. They huddled together as the KV-I heavy tank sent another round into the Panther, the ammunition inside going off like fireworks. Tracers raced over the sky as the Panther burst open, burning. The Germans had won the day, but were now so bled out they could do little else than hold their positions. There were no replacements for the armor and men that had been lost.

Captain Heidemann found them walking to the rear. They climbed aboard his tank to ride to their battalion HQ, what was left of it. With the dark, Langer put his crew into an abandoned bunker with orders to get some sleep. He would see what was going to happen next.

On 10 July, the allies invaded Sicily.

At Wolfshanze in East Prussia, the Führer raged at Kluge and Manstein. His eyes sweaty, a noticeable tic playing on his face, he cursed the Italians for lack of spirit and leadership. He knew Sicily was lost and that the next step for the allies would be an invasion of the Italian mainland and into the Balkans.

Turning to Manstein the Führer spoke in a low voice, trying to control the rage that ate at him. "If this happens, our whole southern European flank will be threatened. That I cannot let happen. It is necessary that we reinforce our units in Italy, and to do that I will have to pull divisions back from the battle for Kursk. There is no other place I can get them. It is my order then that Operation Citadel be stopped."

While the Führer conferred with his generals, Langer sat on the ground outside a Russian *izba* (hut), one of the few left standing. Heidemann tried to gather what remained of his unit into a cohesive force. They were scattered all over the battlefield. Of the twenty he started with, only nine tanks remained and these were in sore need of repairs and fuel.

Breaking away from his radio, he took out a bottle of cherished Calvados brandy from the happier days in France. Pulling the cork with his teeth, he took a long pull of the hot, sweet, apple-flavored brandy. Wiping his lips, he handed it to Langer.

"Look like you could use a pull."

Langer nodded wearily, his face looking as if he were getting ready for a minstrel show. Only the eyes and mouth were clear of soot and dirt. Leaning his head back, he opened his throat and let the sweet burning slide down to his stomach, where it settled in a warm glow.

"It was a bitch out there today, Captain. What's next? Do I get a new tank?"

Heidemann laughed bitterly, "New tank, new tank. There's not a new tank to be had. Until you reach Berlin, this is it. Nine fucking Panthers out of twenty and I don't know what's going to happen next. Until someone at command makes some sense out of this mess, you'll just have to tag along as best you can. There's nothing I can do for you unless you can find your own tank somewhere. You'll just have to join in with the infantry for the time being. Now go back to your crew and get some rest. Scavenge whatever weapons you can find, especially MGs. If Ivan hits us tonight, we'll need everything we have just to make it through the first attack. Now get out of here."

Langer sent Gus and Stefan off to scrounge what they could from the smoking hulks that lay around them. A belt of machine-gun ammo here, a bag of grenades there, a half-buried loaf of bread with only a little mold on one end that could easily be cut off.

Somewhere, Gus came up with three bottles of vodka. Speaking as low as he could, he said to Carl, "You did say the captain said we would have to walk unless we found our own tank didn't you?"

Langer took a pull from one of the bottles. "That's right, you great hulking ape, and the only good thing about it is at least we'll be in the open and I won't have to smell you fart all day."

Gus sucked his lower lip thoughtfully. It was impossible to insult him. "All right, Sarge. Thanks." He walked off looking like a gorilla in uniform.

"Where the hell do you think you are going?" Langer shouted.

"To follow orders, *Herr Feldwebel*, naturally."

Langer was too tired to argue or question him further. Almost without realizing it, his eyes closed. Teacher took the still smoldering cigaret from his fingers and crushed it.

CHAPTER SEVEN

The crackle of a machine gun firing snapped his eyes open. His hand instinctively wrapped around the pistol grip of his submachine gun. Yuri touched him gently on the shoulder. "*Russki charoscho.*"

Pulling up to the edge of the shell hole that had been his bed, Langer wiped sleep from his eyes. They burned and felt sticky. "Where are they coming from?"

Yuri pointed to a darker shadow, barely visible in the night. Another clatter of light machine-gun fire winked at them with bright flashes. Teacher moved up next to him and sighted with his rifle.

Langer pushed the barrel down with his right hand. "No firing. They're just trying to see where our positions are. Pass the word. No firing until I say. If they can't get us to give ourselves away, they'll probably send out a scouting party next. So everyone on his toes and awake. Where's Gus?"

Teacher shrugged in the dark. "I don't know. After you went to sleep, I saw him rambling off to the right mumbling something about following orders."

Carl cursed, anger building. "God damn him. Won't that son of a bitch ever learn to sit still. Yuri, go take a look see." Handing Yuri his watch with an illuminated dial, he pointed to the minute hand and showed Yuri how long to be gone. "Twenty minutes, no more."

Yuri gave one short "*Da, Hetman,*" and then slid on his belly over the shell hole and disappeared.

The minutes crawled. Sweat ran down his back, sticking to his jacket and skin. His armpits felt raw where dried sweat and salt had collected in the hairs, rubbing him raw. Finally, a small dark form wiggled back into the hole silently. Reluctantly he handed the watch back to Langer.

"They come, maybe twenty *moujiks*, peasants. They have a green cross with them. He wants prisoner for question, threaten them with *Piljudji*, prison. They no get." Yuri spat a gob of phlegm on the ground. "NKVD *sabaka* dog."

Calling the others to him, Langer told them to keep quiet and let Ivan get closer, then use knives and entrenching tools first and not to fire unless things became too hairy and they couldn't handle them. The night grated on their ears as they strained for any sound that meant the Ivans were getting near, each man with his favorite weapon for close fighting. Teacher strapped his bayonet to the side of his boot. Putting a finer edge to the blade, Stefan preferred an entrenching tool, the short

67

shovel with the edges sharpened. Yuri played with his butcher knife while Langer picked up an abandoned rifle and fixed his bayonet to it. Manny did the same, following Langer's suggestion that he didn't have enough experience for anything shorter. They waited . . . each man to himself, with his own thoughts.

Teacher mused on how often they got back to the basics of existence and struggle here. Surrounded by all the technology of modern warfare they now waited to beat the brains out of their enemy or gut him with bayonets and butcher knives. Progress marches on.

Yuri hissed softly between his teeth and pointed out into the darkness. Following his finger, Langer could see shadows moving slowly, carefully feeling their way in the darkness between the grass and small brush that remained after the battle. One and then another. *Yuri*, he thought, that little shit has eyes sharper than a jungle cat. Tapping Teacher, he told him to pass the word to get ready.

They hunched lower in the shell hole, only eyes showing above the lip. The first Russian gingerly crept to the edge of the shell hole. Thinking it vacant, he started to crawl in and was helped along with a hand from Langer as his throat was locked in a vise grip. Carl dragged him down to the bottom and squeezed, feeling the cartilage crumble beneath his fingers. There could be no noise. Yuri patted him approvingly on the shoulder when he rose from the Russian's body and went back to the side of the shell hole and regained his rifle and bayonet. Another crept close to Stefan, only to have his head caved in with a blow from the sharpened edge of his shovel. The Russian died, not hearing his last breath, but his comrades immediately behind him heard the sucking sound of the shovel being pulled from his skull. They froze.

The NKVD with the green cross on his soft cap moved up to them. Hearing what happened he reminded them to take prisoners. On his command they were to throw themselves in the hole with the Fascists and wipe them out, except for one, who he would question later. He relished the idea of the screams he would induce when he hammered a brass cartridge into the kneecap of the prisoner. That never failed to elicit a proper response when he asked his questions.

Creeping from one man to another, he made his way down line. When he stood, they were to rush. No shooting. Knives and bayonets only in the hole. There couldn't be too many in a hole that size. Gathering himself, he took a deep breath and then rose to a half stand. His men immediately lunged for the hole. The first one in died with his throat torn open by Yuri's butcher knife, but the others made it in. Langer thrust with the bayonetted rifle like a spear, catching the first one in the stomach and then twisting the blade to tear it free and striking another in the face, crushing the jaw. A bayonet on a Moisin Nagant slid along his rib cage. Burning, he twisted and kicked his attacker in the balls, slashing across his throat as he did. The shell hole was a confused million, grunting, groaning mass of men who stabbed and beat at each other in the dark. Not a word was spoken. They fought and died silently except for the sounds that blades and rifle butts made when they sank into an abdomen or smashed open a skull. The NKVD man threw himself on a German's back and sank his knife deep into him, twisting the blade and moving it from side to side. He felt a sexual thrill as the German's death shudder was transmitted to him from the steel. Turning to take out another one, he lunged at a stocky figure only to have his thrust blocked. A distant flare lit up the hole enough for him to get a quick look at the German, a sergeant with a thin scar on one side of his face running down to the cheek. He lunged again, this time only to feel his hand locked in a grip which bent it back over his wrist. The bones in his wrist cracked as he was thrown to the ground. The last thing he saw was the shadow of the German's boot coming down as Langer kicked his head into a pulp.

The surviving Russians dropped their weapons and began to run back to where they had come from. In the heat of the battle no one had noticed the rumbling clanking that was coming closer to them.

A tank . . .

Teacher swore, "Ah, now we're in for it. Those bastards are going to grind us under. We better get our asses out of here."

The surviving Russians ran to meet the approaching monster only to freeze in terror when it turned and ground three of them under the treads. A gurgling laugh came to Langer's group in the hole. Gus in a Tiger was joyfully chasing the Russians across the field. Only two got away by playing

70

dead, one had his arm flattened out as fifty-six tons of the Tiger ran over it. There was no pain, the sheer weight of the tank pinched all the nerves in the arm.

Gus locked his left tread and headed for the hole, where he wheeled the monster around and leapt from the driver's hatch. Grinning hugely he waddled over to the hole. "What are you doing down there? Come up and see what Uncle Gus has brought you."

Teacher told him to shut up. He was pulling Stefan out from under a pile of Russian bodies. Gus did just that. Getting into the hole, he took Stefan from him and told the others that he would take care of him. For the first time since Langer had known Gus, he had nothing wise or smart ass to say. Taking a shelter half, he wrapped the body in it and carried it off in his arms like a baby. Carl wasn't sure, but thought he heard him crying. *No, not Gus. He wouldn't do that.*

With the dawn, Gus returned. He had carried Stefan seven miles to the rear to the graves registration company in charge of casualties for this sector. After turning Stefan's paybook and ID tags over to them, he had insisted on burying him by himself. He wanted to make sure the job was done right. When he returned, there was no sign that anything had ever happened. He thumped down in the hole and began to wolf down his iron rations, eating as if that was the only thing of importance in the world.

Langer walked around the Tiger noting the deathshead insignia of the Totenkopf Division on the rear and front glacis. Joining Gus, he said,

"Where the hell did you get it?"

Gus, his mouth full, gulped and swallowed, his Adam's apple doing filthy things to his throat. "Well, you said the captain said we should get our own tank. I went and got one and it's a beauty, fully gassed and loaded."

Langer shook his head. "But how?"

Gus smiled a crooked, self-pleased grin. "I knew that bunch of Hitler's cowboys were not too far away, so I paid them a friendly visit to promote brotherly feelings between the SS and the Wehrmacht and to demonstrate my affection for the baby butchers. I took two bottles of vodka with me, but it seems somehow that the mineral oil I use on my hair got into the bottles and the mixture upset the dear boys' stomachs and while they were shitting their guts out, I merely got in and drove off. By the way, I would recommend you find some paint and do some redecorating on it before they come around. They ought to be getting better about now."

Langer climbed into the commander's seat. "Let's move out and find some paint for this mobile pillbox before we have company."

Yuri was now a full-fledged member of the crew and took over the loaders job and Manny moved over to the hull gun and radio.

Gus started up the engine and they headed over to where Captain Heidemann was raising hell with the supply officer about his allotment of petrol and munitions. When the Tiger stopped in front of him, Langer jumped down. The captain stood for a moment stuttering and then, "Where the hell did you get that? No, I don't want to know. Tell me nothing."

Gus stuck his head up through the hatch and winked at Heidemann. Heidemann turned his back. "I didn't see it. It was never here and one of these days, I'm going to have that insubordinate bandit driving for you shot. Now get it out of here and meet us back at Prokhorovka. We are going to regroup there and for God's sake, stay out of the way of the SS. If they see you in one of their tanks, they'll turn you over to the headhunters for target practice. Now go!"

Langer left Heidemann mumbling to himself as they headed off across the field. Gus was happy as a child with a new train set as he played with his toy, all the time keeping Manny informed of the best way to cook a hog's head and keep the flavor in.

CHAPTER EIGHT

Stopping a kilometer outside Prokhorovka in an orchard, Langer was getting ready to send Gus in to get some paint so they could redo the camouflage and put on their battalion markings when Gus let out a yelp of joy. Walking in the open was one of the women's mortar crews.

Spotting the Tiger facing them, they froze and slowly put up their hands. The woman commanding the crew was all that Gus had dreamed of, massive tits that bulged the front of her drab uniform to the bursting point and legs like tree stumps sitting in high leather boots. Gus rushed her crying out, "*Ya Cheybya Loobloo Djavuschka*, I love you girls."

Sergeant Tina Yurenova caught the look in his eyes and took off, tank or no tank. She ran into the orchard dodging between trees, Gus racing after her giving off cries of passion concerning her *Alik* (sexual organs). "Don't run from Uncle Gus, my little pigeon." He caught her tunic with one square-fingered hand and she turned and slugged him square in the face, crossing his eyes.

"She loves me," he cried and began tearing the clothes off her.

Langer and the others merely stared in amazement. Teacher started to stop him but Carl said to leave him alone. "When he's in heat he just might turn his attention to you. Besides, I'm not sure if she can't whip him in a fair fight."

Tina Yurenova defended herself and her honor from the assault of this human tank. She kicked, clawed and fought, trying to knee him in the balls, but all to no avail, and soon all that was left on her were her boots. Gus was on her, the two floundering in the trees and grass, resembling two pink pigmy dinosaurs. They grappled, grunting and squealing, Tina Yurenova threatening to feed Gus his balls when Russia won the war. She kicked and cursed. The bushes shook until Langer thought the roots were going to be torn up. Suddenly the screams and curses stopped and gurgles of pleasure began to emerge. He caught a quick glimpse of fleshy white thighs over black boots, heels drumming the ground. A feminine giggle seemed out of place coming from the mouth of this woman. Her giggles were punctuated by roars of laughter from Gus as he demonstrated the merits of the German helmet. Soon both were completely involved, oblivious to anything else. Twice Gus tried to get up, only to be dragged back into the bushes. After what seemed to be hours, the two emerged stark naked, holding hands like teenagers, Yurenova's head on Gus's shoulder. Looking up she saw the rest of the crew watching her and ran back into the bushes to dress. She tossed Gus his uniform. While he was getting his trousers back on, Gus told Langer she promised to get him a job in a tractor factory in Ryazhsk where her brother was a foreman if he would desert. "Do you think I should?"

Teacher merely looked at him as if he were the personification of every base instinct known to mankind. "No," said Langer, "I don't think it's a love match that would endure. Now get your ass into town and find me some paint or I'll have your guts for suspenders." Gus looked back at his lady love. "Don't worry," Carl said. "We'll let them go. Now move it!"

Gus complied unwillingly and trotted off down the road. As the women disappeared from sight, Teacher asked, "What do you think they'll do to her for collaborating with the enemy?"

Langer chuckled. "They'll probably give her the Order of Lenin. I'm sure by now she's told the others she sacrificed her honor to save them from the same horrible fate and that she only pretended to enjoy it for their sakes."

Teacher lit up his pipe, thought for a moment and then dismissed them from his mind with one statement. "You're probably right, but sometimes Gus worries me."

Three hours later, Gus was back, riding a motorcycle with a side car and inside enough paint to do three tanks.

"Where did you get the motorcycle?" Then, imitating Heidemann's response, "Never mind, I don't want to know. Just leave it in the trees."

The rest of the day was spent turning their new Tiger I into a different tank, which was fortunate because shortly after they had finished and the paint barely dry, two SD headhunters came by in a *Kübelwagen* asking if they had seen a Tiger with Totenkopf markings on it go by lately, being driven by a maniac who said he was with the 7th Panzer Division. Gus had an angelic expression on his face as he told them he had seen one earlier and pointed to a distant ridge to the north. The headhunters thanked him and wheeled their vehicle around, bounced off and headed in the direction indicated.

Langer stood confused for a moment and then turned to Teacher after checking his map. "Isn't that the ridge we bypassed yesterday where the Russian antitank guns were dug in?"

The sound of the Kübelwagen exploding answered the question for him. Gus just smiled and said, "Well, are we going to hang around here all day? Let's get on into town. It's about suppertime and I spotted a field kitchen while there that bears looking into." The smoke from the burning Volkswagen jeep sent up one lonely black tendril behind them as their new home clanked on the dirt road to join the rest of their unit.

In Prokhorovka, Heidemann said nothing as they rumbled in. As far as he was concerned, they were still riding a Panther. In the next few days, the front collapsed as divisions were moved out of the line for transfer to Italy. Gus moaned at the thought of others going to Rome. He was going to miss the food and the women. He cursed fate for leaving him behind.

Every hour the Russian pressure became greater. The Germans fought a running battle as they withdrew, making Ivan pay for every step, but Ivan always seemed to have more men than they had bullets and by 15 July, they were in a defensive perimeter outside Kharkov. The city itself was burned out. Only a shell was left from the fighting that had taken place when the Germans captured it the last time.

Teacher fell in love with the Tiger's 88 mm gun. It fired a twenty-two-pound shell at 2,657 feet per second, heavy enough and fast enough to cut the turret of a T-34 like butter. It was slower, but the increased armor gave them a feeling of security. They were positioned near a battery of 88 mm flak guns which could serve dual purpose as antitank. Between them they had accounted for fourteen enemy tanks in the last three days without getting a scratch on their paint, but Ivan was keeping the pressure on them, bringing up an ever increasing amount of artillery and "Stalin organs" firing those horrendous barrages night and day.

General Voronezh massed two infantry armies, the 5th and 6th Guards, along with two tank armies packed into a front of no more than two miles, backed up with the support of 370 pieces of artillery per mile of front. The tanks had a depth of 100 to the mile. To the north, Koniev was to attack Belgorod and then move southwards and hit Kharkov and also keep army detachment Kempf from being able to lend any support to the defenders.

The Germans were down to only 300,000 men in the pocket. The Soviets had them outmanned and out gunned and out tanked by at least three to one. Day after day, Langer's men faced wave after wave of Red soldiers throwing themselves into the fire of the German guns mindless of losses. They would come again and again and every day there were fewer familiar faces around them and no new ones to take their places. On 22 August, Field Marshal Manstein ordered the city evacuated counter to Hitler's orders. Langer and his crew withdrew through burning buildings and exploding supply dumps. The city was to be destroyed and nothing would be left behind for the Russians to use. The sounds of the explosions rumbled all that day and night as the city died for the second time. Units leapfrogging each other kept the Russian bear at bay while they withdrew, destroying everything.

There was little left of the city of Kharkov except a smoldering mass of rubble. The flames could be seen for fifty miles in any direction. Kharkov had been the third largest city in Russia. Behind them the retreating Germans did leave one thing— 133,000 men had been lost. Kharkov, the old-timers knew, was the beginning of the end.

Langer's Tiger moved with the rest of a long line of hundreds of armored vehicles and trucks, passing horse-drawn wagons filled with supplies and the wounded. They moved back. Heidemann, his tank and the two others were all that remained. The strain was on every face, thin, drawn and exhausted. The weariness reached into the bones and men marched while asleep, stumbling caricatures of their former glory—ragged and tired they marched with the steps of men old before their time, trying to keep the blind fear of panic from their minds. They would stop at the Dnieper two hundred kilometers to the west. There they would stand and fight again on what was called the Wotan Line. Wotan, the ancient German god of war.

Langer slept in his seat. The others curled up where they could. The outside of the tank was covered with infantrymen and the survivors of a Luftwaffe antiaircraft crew that had been overrun. Everyone was heading west, a line of men and machines one hundred kilometers long. The air force did its best to provide air cover and keep the Yaks, MIGs and Shtormoviks off them, but every day the burning hulks of tanks and trucks marked the way to the river. Several times they had to stop and fight a rear-guard action to keep Ivan from rolling them up. When at last they reached the crossing at Dniepropetrovsk and passed over the muddy waters, they collapsed and slept where they fell.

CHAPTER NINE

In the wake of the retreating German forces came the others, civilians, cattle, goats and herds of sheep and horses; everything that could move under its own power walked. The industrial machinery of the region was loaded onto trains and hauled back, everything from threshing machines to damaged tractors and tanks, anything that could be put into service of the Reich later, and at the same time deny the Bolsheviks the use of them.

As they withdrew, many divisions took Hitler's orders literally, "Scorched earth—leave nothing for the enemy!" The men evacuated were the technicians and those of gun-bearing age. For the Russians, that meant anyone from fourteen to sixty that could walk. Old men were especially useful in the first waves of assault for locating minefields. . . .

Escorting this menagerie of animals and humanity were many of the *Freiwillegen* (volunteer) units, Turkomen from Asian Russia and mounted detachments of Cossack cavalry from the Caucasus. Ukrainian police along with the members of the Red Cross from Hungary, Romania, and Slovakia were mixed into the fleeing masses all looking to one thing, the river. There they would find safety from the pursuing Russian horses trying to cut them off.

First priority went to the hundred thousand wounded soldiers of the Reich. These were evacuated in the rail cars and trucks; none were left behind. After all, they would be needed later when they could fight again. The others would have to take their chances.

The command was given by the *Ober Kommand Des Wehrmacht* that everything in front of the river for a distance of twelve to twenty-five miles was to be destroyed down to the last house and barn. Forests were to be burned, and bridges blown, as the last of the retreating forces withdrew across them.

For the survival of those left behind, the German Force left one-fifth of the foodstuffs, though this did the civilians little good, as these stores were immediately confiscated for the use of the Red Army. Of the forty-three tanks of Heidemann's company, only seven survived the maelstrom of Kursk and Kharkov, only forty-two men and junior officers answered the roll call. The rest were dead or on their way to slave labor camps beyond the Urals. Heidemann was the senior officer and his remnants were assigned as an ad hoc reserve force as they no longer existed as a regiment or even a company.

A smile broke through the dust caking Heidemann's face and dimmed eyes when he saw the scarred face of Langer sticking up from the hatch of his Tiger I. They had lost contact since the evacuation of Kharkov, and personally he was glad to see the last of the burning refuse pile they had left behind. Three times now he had fought his way in and out of the city and had lost too many good men in the process. Perhaps this would be the last of it, Kharkov was a curse for armor. Tanks belonged where they could use their mobility to lunge deep behind the enemy rear and strike, like the horse cavalry of old, in daring penetrations that could spread panic all out of proportion to the actual threat. Just the thought of an enemy to your rear was terrifying. More than once a couple of lost German tanks had blundered unwittingly into a Russian headquarters area. The resulting confusion of the wildly firing tanks trying only to get out of there had been enough to start a frantic retreat, as whole divisions withdrew from the front lines in panic when they heard that their HQ was being attacked by Panzers.

Heidemann tossed Langer a sack of army bread only four days old and two large cheeses that had seen better days. "Sorry, this is all there is, supplies will take a while to straighten out. After all, they have to have the proper requisition forms, you know. Hunger is not reason enough for the machinery of the German army to grant one something to eat."

Langer yelled something unintelligible down to Gus, who stuck his head up through the driver's hatch mumbling. He climbed out and then leaned back in grunting, his pants showing a large plaid patch on the ass. He hauled up a couple of sacks and tossed them down to the feet of Heidemann. Jumping down to stand in front of him he clicked his heels, brought his arm up in the Hitler-style salute, bellowing at the top of his lungs. "Sir, *Obergefreiter* Gustav Beidemann begs to report that he has, using the initiative ordained in the book of Holy German Army regulations, section 23-2 sub paragraph 765-b, prevented certain items from falling into the hands of the godless sub-human Bolsheviks, which I present to Herr Hauptmann as regulations require for his disposal of, Sir!" With a moué of distaste, Heidemann returned the salute in the army manner and kicked the sacks.

"You know Gus," Carl said. "When Kharkov was burning we came across a supply truck loaded with all the necessities of life for the general officers' mess. It had a busted axle so Gus shoved it out of the way with the Tiger, and in exchange for giving the driver a ride out of the town, we loaded up with enough general-type food and booze to last for a couple of weeks."

Heidemann gave Gus a dirty look. "What happened to the truck? You know the penalty that will come down when the brass finds their chow is gone!"

Gus smirked. "No problem, *Herr Haputmann*. Teacher put a round from the eighty-eight into the truck and it became just one more casualty of the greater war against Bolshevism."

In spite of himself, Captain Heidemann couldn't repress a grin. "All right, Langer, you take your animals and get to a place you can cover the bridge from." Picking up the sacks he looked at Gus still standing at rigid attention. "Beidemann, you are without a doubt the most obnoxious, ill-disciplined and insubordinate bastard I have ever met in my life." His bags clanked as he slung them over his shoulder.

"Thanks."

Before September ended the crossings at Cherkassy, Kremenchug, Dnepropetrovsk and Kanev had been in use day and night. Manstein's forces poured through these fragile channels and deployed to right and left, taking up positions on what was now to be called "The Eastern Rampart."

The Russians ignored German propaganda claims that they would be destroyed at the banks of the Dnieper and continued to overrun German rear-guard units at will until on the twenty-first advance, elements of Vatutin's 3rd Guards Army reached the banks of the river and three days later had already established several small bridgeheads on the opposite banks where the German forces were spread too thin to effectively oppose them. During this phase the Germans had only one minor success. Vatutin ordered the 1st, 3rd and 5th Guards Parachute Brigades to be dropped on the German side of the Dnieper to reinforce the Soviet bridgeheads and to also block the advances of any German reinforcements. Their timing was a little off. The 1st and 3rd missed their DZ and the 10th

Panzer Grenadier Division having moved in the night before was directly under them when the 5th Guards made their jump. The 5th Guards were promptly torn to pieces by the Grenadiers, many of them while still hanging in the sky from their parachutes. Less than two thousand of the nearly eight thousand men dropped survived the next few days to join up with partisan forces in the area. The rest were hunted down and killed or captured.

Langer returned from Heidemann's HQ with the word they were to load up and move out. They were to head north a few kilometers and lend support to a battalion of Jagers that faced a section of the river where it narrowed.

"All right, Teacher, get the others together and take this thing," referring to the Tiger, "over to the depot and load up with everything you can get your hands on. If there's any problem, let Gus do the negotiating. I'll meet you there a little later. I've got to figure out our route on this." He took a Russian road map out of his jacket. "I don't know how the Russians ever find us if they're using their own charts."

CHAPTER TEN

Teacher watched the broad back of his tank commander as he heaved one 88 mm shell after another up to Gus. Gus handed them to Yuri, who stuck them into the holding racks. Langer was as strong as anyone he had ever seen for his size. He never seemed to suffer from the almost chronic conditions of diarrhea which hounded most armies in the field. Bad water, bad food, bad schnapps, nothing seemed to upset him for long. What was there about him that picked at the edges of his mind? Why did Langer live when others died? There was the time when they had been overrun by Siberians and Carl had been hit in the gut. Teacher had seen enough wounds to know that the one Langer received should have been fatal. From the entry point of the bullet it should have torn his liver in two. They had left him for dead—no pulse, no sign of breath, no eye reflex. Langer was dead. But two days later he showed up again apparently none the worse for his wound, only complaining a little about minor stomach pains.

Langer's explanation was that the bullet had entered and exited cleanly, leaving only a puncture. Always sounded somewhat implausible to him, but they had been too busy staying in front of Ivan to worry much. They were glad enough to have him back no matter what the reason. Not until later did Teacher try to analyze it, and it never made sense. The wound Langer had was a killing one, at best even if it had entered and left cleanly, it would still have torn him up inside from the shock wave effect that a high-velocity bullet always has on human tissue.

Teacher considered himself to be well educated and versed in history, which he taught in the Gymnasium in Cologne. But Langer would come out every now and then with a fragment of information that only scholars of ancient history would have been familiar with. His ability to speak languages, even that of Yuri. He also knew the man's customs. Sometimes he spoke of the past as if it had just happened. Like the first winter of the retreat from Moscow. Teacher had told him he thought it must be as cold as when Napoleon had to retreat.

Langer had, offhandedly, said simply, "No, it was colder then."

A statement of fact, no more, no less, said with the conviction of one who knows for sure what he is talking about.

∘ ∘ ∘

Gus shifted into neutral as Carl called down, "What the hell's going on? Where do you think you're going?"

"TANKS!" a youngster yelled back, panic at the edge of his voice. "The Russians are crossing the river! They've built a bridge just under the surface, and they're coming across, hundreds of them, Siberians!"

Langer forced the young corporal to climb on the tank with him, along with three other men, and guided them to the crossing. Manny tried to raise HQ on the radio, but all he got was static.

Teacher checked his 88, and Yuri took his position. He was ready to hand up, from the ammo racks, whichever shell might be needed, as they rumbled on toward the Russian penetration.

A short burst from the hull gun convinced the increasing numbers of fleeing soldiers that it would be wiser to return to their positions and face the oncoming Siberians than to be ground under the treads of their own tanks. From the expression on the tank commander's face, they had no doubt that that was exactly what he would do if they didn't obey his orders.

The massive steel leviathan escorting them helped to return some of their courage; they were soldiers again, not a fleeing mass of panic-stricken men.

A shadow loomed in the dark, and the Tiger's instant response blew the T-34 into a burning hulk, before Ivan had even spotted them.

The sight of the burning tank gave the German infantry new heart, and they moved forward under the protection of the Tiger's 88. Others from the dark woods began to join them, forming into groups, weapons at the ready. They were hunched figures flickering in the flames of the burning Russian tank.

Another T-34 came at them from the side, crashing out of the tree line, firing. Its 76 mm round hit the Tiger's turret at an angle; and even though they were no more than fifty meters apart, the shell ricocheted off to explode in the distance. Trees prevented the Tiger's crew from maneuvering or turning its gun to face the attacker.

The young corporal, who had been so terrified just moments before, leaped off the Tiger and ran to meet the advancing Russian. Halting by the body of one of the Pioneers that had been with him, he took the man's demolitions bag and opened it while running and twisting through the trees. When he tossed the bag away he held in his hands a *geballte Ladung:* a bundled charge of six grenade heads taped around the head of a complete stick grenade. Throwing himself to the earth in front of the T-34, he let the monster move over him as he had been taught at the training school at Kaiserslautern, and the steel bottom scraped his helmet as it passed. Immediately the youngster rose, pulled the igniter on the bundle charge, tossed it on the tank's rear deck, and threw himself to the side seeking shelter in the roots of trees.

The *geballte* blew with enough force to wreck the engine compartment, leaving the T-34 unable to move, but still dangerous. Its guns continued to fire and sweep over the Germans on the trail. The Russian crew fired and loaded faster than they had ever done in their lives.

A *Stabsgefreiter* from the Pioneers took advantage of the tank's blind spots and set a magnetic mine at the junction of hull and turret. Then he threw himself down beside the corporal, burying his face in the earth.

The Soviet monster died in less than a beat of a heart when the mine blew the turret open and exploded the ammo inside. The Germans had no time to congratulate themselves before their backs were ripped open by bursts from PPs 41s. The Russian infantry support was catching up, but without the aid of their comrades in the dead tank, the Germans made short work of them. With the aid of the Tiger's hull machine guns, Gus had finally worked the Tiger around where it could trace the enemy's route back.

The Russians hadn't fully exploited the river crossing. One of their tanks had stalled on the underwater bridge, and the others were lined up behind it, trying to push it off of the side when Langer's Tiger came on the scene. The Ivans were being aided in their effort to clear the bridge by Langer, when a round from his 88 blew the stalled tank clear from the bridge. Cursing as he realized his mistake in blasting the sitting duck free so that the others could come on, he fired again at the leading tank, aiming for the treads.

"FIRE!"

The round blew the Russian half on and half off the bridge. The crossing was barred again.

One T-34 after another was knocked out. After

they hit the leading tank, he took out the rear. That left eight more stuck in the center, unable to advance or withdraw. One by one they fell prey to the pinpoint fire of the lone Tiger opposing them. The German infantry was mopping up the few Siberians that had managed to get across. No prisoners were taken, they didn't have the time or the men to spare for such niceties. That, along with what their fellows suffered at the hands of the wild Asians, made their choice easy. . . .

The opposite bank of the river burst into flashes of fire and smoke. Shells by the hundreds began to fall among the milling mass of Russian tanks that had been awaiting their turn to line up for the crossing. These monsters had been unable to lend any support to their comrades on the bridge. When Russian intelligence selected this site they did so because of the narrow defile leading to the crossing. It would aid in keeping their vehicles from being spotted from the air or opposite bank. This choice now made the defile a mass grave for hundreds of men as the combined artillery of three German batteries poured onto them. Someone had got through to HQ with the coordinates of the Russian attack, and was now calling down accurate fire on the congested Russian column. This attempt had been stopped, but there would be others.

Three days later, Field Marshal Eric von Manstein conferred the Knight's Cross on *Stabsfeldwebel* Langer, commander of the tank crew, and the Iron Cross first class on the rest of the crew.

Hanging the ribbon with its dangling cross around the sergeant's neck, the aristocratic field marshal gave the awardee a long strange look, as if there was something in the man's face that he was supposed to see, but somehow had missed.

The small formation had not been dismissed ten minutes before Gus was trying to sell his medal to a newly arrived member of a supporting Pioneer battalion which had been assigned to their area. Manfried was ecstatic with the thought of how proud his father would be. Teacher merely gave his to Yuri. The Tatar had been omitted at the ceremony, and Teacher didn't really give a rat's ass for any piece of tin; all he wanted from the war was out.

Autumn soon came with its changing colors and hints of the snow that lay not far behind. The fields and trees were glorious in the kaleidoscope of colors that preceded the advent of the Russian winter.

The Russians continued their attempts to break through the forces on the Dnieper time and again. It seemed that they had a never-ending supply of men and material to throw against the defenders, who had less to resist them with every day. The snows came and gave the landscape a deceptive look of peace and tranquility. The snow, a clean white sheet, covered the horrors of thousands of decaying bodies of men and horses; and it turned the burned-out shells of tanks into small white hills that dotted the landscape as far as the eye could see. . . .

CHAPTER ELEVEN

From that time on, until the first blast of November, they served as a fire brigade in one savage confrontation after another. Twice their Tiger had to be taken in for repairs that they couldn't handle in the fields; once for a complete engine overhaul, and another time to have the transversing rings and rollers replaced. Other than that they had been lucky. But another winter was coming now; and flurries of snow in the morning and evening were harbingers of the white death that would soon sweep down on them. True, they were fairly well outfitted with winter gear and felt boots like those of the Russians, but their equipment wasn't designed with the tolerances of their Soviet counterparts. Their guns would still freeze up, the oil in the breeches would lock solid, trucks and cars that stopped in bad weather would have their blocks frozen solid, and men would die of carbon monoxide poisoning from trying to sleep in their vehicles while keeping the motors running.

The battalion was reformed. The faces of the re-placements were younger every year, indeed every month. Faces like Manny's that would soon look older than their years, especially their eyes, old men's eyes in eighteen-year-old faces.

Nikopol was to their front about three or four kilometers, and just to the rear was the encampment of the Kalmyks. They, along with Heidemann's unit, had been assigned to the defense of Nikopol. The Kalmyks, along with their families, had fought fiercely alongside the Germans ever since 1942. They hated the Russians with a savagery that even the SS couldn't match.

They had left the Kalmyk steppes, with their wives and families driving their herds of horses before them. Now they served as scouts, and they specialized in rooting out partisans. They had stayed with the 16th Panzers all the way, and thought of the division as their own personal property and family, something to defend at all costs. They, and Heidemann, were under the command of General of Mountain Troops, Ferdinand Schorner.

The German forces held a bridgehead in an arc seventy-five kilometers across. Behind them ran the Dnieper, and on their southern flank was the Plavna, a swamp covering a larger area than their own perimeter; these swampy lowlands were the haunts of the partisans. Without the aid of the half-savage Kalmyk cavalry units, it would have been almost impossible to control the guerrillas in the morass of reeds and marsh.

Here they waited, fighting and dying until

Father Winter finally proclaimed his mastery over the land. The great cold had come, and like the animals, those that could bury themselves in the earth did so to seek whatever shelter and warmth they could. Anything to keep out of the icy wind that froze a man's feet into blackened stumps, and sapped the will to live until one just sat down and quit, waiting for the peace that would come with freezing. Freezing wasn't so bad; the old-timers said that after a while you couldn't feel the cold, and then for a short time you were actually warm, and that was when death would come. . . .

Langer sat, his eyes barely showing over the lip of the open turret hatch, trying to pierce the darkness. They were out there; every instinct told him that they were coming. It had been too quiet for the last few days, only scouting patrols had been intercepted. It was too quiet! Now he took the watch just before the hours of dawn, Ivan's favorite time to attack. That was when the body in sleep or repose took the longest time to get awake, when seconds meant the difference between life and death. His eyes blanked out. *"Flares!"*

The sounds reached him split seconds later, but he was already inside the hatch. The Russian barrage lit up the night, one long continuous rolling wave of fiery destruction. It rumbled across the frozen earth. It rolled over them, missing the sitting Tiger. Only the *spaaang* of ricocheting shrapnel told them how close they had come to being destroyed.

The radio crackled, Heidemann's voice breaking in. "All Panzers, start engines and move out, give support to the infantry, but don't tie yourselves down. If you have to leave them, we can't afford to lose any more armor. This is the Breakout: follow plan 'C' to rendezvous; you're on your own, Ivan is hitting us too." The crackling of the radio stopped, there was no need for anything more to be said.

General Schorner had been expecting this, and contrary to Hitler's orders of "Fight to the last man," he preferred to risk his own life and disobey the suicide orders to save his men. Strangely enough, the order for Breakout was, "Ladies, excuse me, please."

From the north, General Chuykov's 8th Guards Army assaulted the rear of the bridgehead. It was the night of 31 January.

Langer's Tiger patrolled like a hungry wolf between the retreating German forces and the Russians hounding them, trying to keep the Soviet armor off their back until they could break contact. Four times they had sent screeching rounds into advancing Russian tanks, sending them and their crews to eternity.

Everything was in confusion until they could join the main force between the river and Apostolovo. There the situation stabilized, as the German units added their strength to those already there. The uncommon warm spell of the last week had turned the ground from ice to the knee-deep clinging mud that bogged down tanks and trucks. Infantrymen had to tie strips of canvas around their legs to keep their boots from being pulled off by the sucking mud.

Exhausted men, who could go no further, died from suffocation when they fell face first into it, sinking out of sight so that their bodies were not seen by those who marched over them.

Langer wrapped his olive-colored scarf around his lower mouth and nose, leaving only the eyes exposed to the whipping, icy wind. Outside the bunker, the shock of the cold snatched his breath. The whirling winds of snow had covered everything in a clean blanket of virgin white that covered, at least for the time, the horrors that lay beneath them. A distant flickering in the sky lit up the darkness, like a burning star. . . .

Flares. The storm was no guarantee that Ivan wouldn't come across the frozen fields. The temperature had dropped from twenty above to forty below zero. He had seen a snap freeze like this once before, during the retreat from Moscow, the cold that comes so fast that you don't know that it's killing you.

He had come upon a small group of Cossacks. The snow was waist high, and several were mounted. For a moment, he started to fire, until he saw that there were no frozen wisps of breath coming from them, or their animals. One of the riders held a cigaret in hand, head bending over slightly, ready to light it with a match that had blown away. All were dead in the act of living. Langer figured that it had happened three days earlier, when a snap freeze came across the plains from Siberia.

That, with the seventy-mile-an-hour winds, brought a chill factor of over a hundred below zero, so cold that it froze the fluids servicing the brain. It came fast, the white death, so fast that you never knew it. As you were, so you died, asleep or awake. This night was like that, not as cold perhaps, but cold enough to kill over a thousand men on both sides before the dawn would come.

Small flickers in the night showed where crews of tanks built small fires under their vehicles to keep the engines from freezing solid. Antifreeze didn't help. Machine gunners heated bricks red hot and put them on the breeches of the weapons to prevent them from locking up if they had to be used. The bricks had to be changed every ten minutes.

Heaving his way through the knee-deep white, breath laboring and aching, he looked for Manny, trying to find his bearings to the outpost. It was only a hundred and fifty meters from the bunker, but it took over twenty minutes to make it, fighting the wind and drifts.

Stooping over, he moved the canvas covering aside, letting a blast of arctic air enter with him. The wind almost blew out the tin-can stove which served only to keep the worst of the cold out. Gus grumbled at the incursion; he was at the aperture, searching out the Russian side of the field through a pair of artillery range-finding glasses. The opening was packed with rags around the lenses, which he had to wipe off every couple of minutes to keep them from icing up.

"Goddamn, Sarge, it's about time! Where is Manny? I thought that he was supposed to relieve me!"

"He never showed?"

Concern erased Gus's habitual cynicism. "No, he

hasn't been here. Then he's still out there!" Gus started to move past Langer and was stopped by a gloved hand.

"No, you stay here. I'll backtrack and see if I can find him. Maybe he holed somewhere with another crew. You stay and keep an eye on the front, unless you feel a desire to have the Siberians play games with you. Remember Moscow. . . ."

Unwillingly, Gus conceded and returned to the lenses. "Find him, Carl, please."

That was the first time, the only time, that Langer had ever heard Gus say please to anyone.

Back in the dark, the wind was trying to cut through to the skin. Ice built up on his eyebrows and collected in the hair of his lids, trying to squeeze them shut and close them forever, as it had done to so many others in this waste of frozen nightmares.

CRUMP! CRUMP! The dull thumping explosions of incoming mortar rounds walked over the earth. Langer threw himself beside a broken tree, sinking down, face forward, into the drift built around the base of the tree the height of a man's waist.

The barrage walked on searching out anything it could kill. Langer rose to his knees, lungs aching, and leaned against the trunk of the shell-wrecked tree.

Something in the shape of the drift piled up on the base of the tree bothered him. A fresh burst of wind came across the fields from the north. A gust blew past his face and whipped at the drift he was looking at, blowing a piece of crust off the top. A helmet top. A coldness gripped his insides, but it wasn't caused by the wind. Using his glove, he wiped away the snow from the helmet and face, knowing what he would find, but hoping that he was wrong. Manny's face stared out from its glowing white cover. The eyes were wide open, his face calm, no trace of fear or of anxiety, looking as if he had just stopped to rest and think for a moment and was forever frozen in that state. Ice crusted around his eyes and mouth made him look older than his nineteen years. Langer moved the rest of the snow from him and picked up what used to be Manfried Ertl. The body was frozen solid in the sitting position. Langer struggled back to the bunker carrying his burden; the wind blew on, uncaring. Manfried was of no importance, only one more to be added to the roll call of the greatest of Russian killers— General Winter. Laying his burden on the snow on its side by the bunker, Langer went inside. There was no need to bring Manny in to thaw. The cold would keep him until they could bury him.

An infantry company of SS, moving up under the cover of darkness, died in its steps. 155 mm shells set to explode in the air picked their spot to do so directly over the SS men. The concussion killed more than shrapnel. The company looked as if they had just lain down to catch some sleep.

Langer and his crew tried to pull themselves deeper into the dirt floor of their bunker. There was nothing they could do to fight back, they just had to take it. They slept only when exhaustion finally claimed them. Even the shaking of the frozen earth was not enough to keep their grime laden eyelids open. They slept unmindful of the hell that raged around them.

Manny's body was no longer a problem; a 105 shell had disposed of it forever.

German sentries on the forward observation posts were the first to know that hell was on its way. From the distance, winking eyes of light joined together until there was one continuous rim of flashing illuminations, setting the horizon on fire. Then came the screaming of the shells. The Russian offensive had begun! Over a thousand pieces of artillery, and hundreds of multiple rocket launchers pounded a three-mile section of the front for five days, twenty-four hours around the clock without cease. Russian gunners and crews worked themselves to death, hearts breaking under the strain of loading their guns with the heavy shells. As they fired, many lost their hearing forever. The shells fell in hundreds and thousands, over a hundred rounds fired for every German in the target area. Men and animals died. The screaming of the horses, wild-eyed and trembling, was worse than that of the men. Eardrums were shattered, blood running from the ears to freeze in blackened clots on the side of the face.

A seventeen-year-old private, who had been on the front for only three days when the barrage began, stuck the muzzle of his Mauser rifle into his mouth and pulled the trigger with the aid of a stick. Many more took his way out of the nightmare. Others by the dozens merely walked away, no longer able to cope. The pounding, interminable concussions ripping their minds apart and sent them

stumbling back slack jawed, hands dangling at their
sides or holding their heads trying to keep out the
sounds. They staggered to the rear, only to find
peace at the hands of the SD. Like children they
cried and obeyed when they were told to kneel, still
holding their hands over their ears to keep out the
sounds of distant thunder. They didn't even hear
the neck shots fired by their comrades that finally
took the nightmares away.

Russians came by the tens of thousands, white
winter camouflage mixed with mustard brown.
They swarmed into the gap, killing the still stunned
Germans by the hundreds before the Fascists even
knew they were there. In their ears they still heard
the thunder. For the Russians, it was inconceivable
that anyone could survive the hell of fire that they
had laid on, much less be able to fight when it
stopped.

But, somehow, men did survive it; and the few
moments of respite they had while the Russians
mopped up the men in front gave those in the rear
time to crawl out of their holes and burrows. Tears
streaming from their faces, black from grime and
filth, stinking filthy apparitions. They came out
with guns in their hands. At last here was something
they could deal with. Many, in their frustration,
beat at the sides of the Russian tanks with riflebutts
and shovels; pounding, striking, anything to hit
back at the terror that had torn them for the last five
days. Like insects they attacked, beating and
screaming at the steel beasts until, when they an-
noyed it too much, it would turn and trample them
under. But many of the beasts died too. Desperate

men fired *Panzerfausts* from twenty feet. Others threw themselves bodily onto the Russian tanks holding mines and sticky bombs; exploding themselves and the Russians, turning both into warm spots on the frozen fields.

Langer raised his head not sure of the silence. Why had the earth stopped shaking? It didn't feel natural. The earth was supposed to tremble and move with the vibrating waves of the barrage. Blood dripping from his nose and ears, he pulled himself out of the bunker, pushing aside fallen planks.

Crawling back inside, he kicked his men into awareness. Cursing and shoving, he forced them out into the open where the habits of years took over. Behaving as automatons, they went about their duties clearing the junk off the Tiger. They climbed inside shutting the hatches.

Gus's face was that of a man about to go mad, but his hands hit the starter switch by themselves. The Maybachs roared into life again. The rumbling gave them some sense of purpose. Teacher loaded and sighted. Yuri sat on the hull MG, his face the only one that showed no sign of strain. Calm, peaceful, ready to kill or die as he had always been. Only he had been able to lose himself inside his own mind and block out the thunder.

"Move out!" Gus's hands and feet moved, sending the eighty tons out of its hole onto the frozen surface. It rose from the ground in time to strike out at the first wave of Russians, mowing them down like fields of wheat beneath the raking fire of the hull MG and that of the turret. Teacher reloaded and fired with HE rounds. There was no way to miss.

Langer raked the field, the heat from the breech of his MG was welcome warmth. He fired, killing men by the dozens, but nothing could stop the Russian advance. Not tanks, not courage, only death could still them, and there were too many. They split the German forces and the tides of battles surged their own way. One took Langer's Tiger to the north until the tank ran out of fuel on the edge of the battlefield. It rested in the thin trees of the edge of a forest. The battle passed them by as it did hundreds of others. Ivan would come back for them later.

Hauptmann Heidemann thrust his Panther in the way of four assaulting KV-Is trying to give a hospital unit a few more seconds to get away with their wounded. He had taken out two when a 76 mm shell tore through the side plating of the turret, cutting his body in half before it exploded in the ammo racks. The Panther burst open to burn for a few minutes and then die.

The hospital was next. The Russians killed them all, wounded or whole made no difference. They drank medical alcohol, raped the few women there and then killed them. *Urra Stalino*, this was war the way they liked it. They had been promised the women of Germany and took them wherever they found them.

CHAPTER TWELVE

"I'm hungry." Gus was back to normal and that one statement broke the tension. Teacher and Langer fell to laughing as Yuri looked with amazement at Gus's yawning maw, down which incredible lengths of blood sausage were disappearing. Gus fascinated him. If he had been from the steppes he would have been a Hetman, a chieftain. There, excess in anything was admired.

Langer dug in his pack and took out a last pack of cigarets, handing one around to each of his men. Teacher tore his in half and stuck half in his pipe.

They emerged from their steel shelter, and stood in the drifts, listening. The sounds of battle were far away and receding, the storm was passing them by, leaving them for the moment, alone.

Without being told, Gus and Yuri began to take their gear out of the Tiger. Personal weapons and food would be all they could take. It might be a long time and way until they rejoined a German unit. More likely Ivan would find them first.

Langer spoke softly. "Teacher, what do you think?"

Stomping his feet to keep the circulation going, he puffed slowly at his pipe. "I don't know, Carl. Only death waits to the south. We might have a better chance of connecting if we go north. Maybe the front's still holding there."

Langer stuck the butt between his lips. Taking a deep drag he held the smoke in his lungs for a moment, enjoying the biting of the fumes.

"I don't know. More than likely Ivan has taken Krivoy Rog. It might be better if we headed northwest to where the railway crosses the Bug. If anything is still holding, it will be there at Pervomaysk. It's a long way, though, old friend."

Teacher nodded. "No further than we have already come. What's another two hundred kilometers? It means nothing, we die here or we die there. What is the difference? We have to all be somewhere, and one place is as good as another for the likes of us."

Gus set booby traps on all the hatches of the sitting Tiger. The first Ivan that peeked in should set off the remaining shells.

Each loaded up and selected what he thought would be of the most use to him on the trek. They had enough food for three days if they used their iron rations; after that it would be whatever they could come across, and that might be damned thin.

Langer ordered Gus to take the turret machine gun and distributed ten of the fifty-round belt drums among the others. Gus grumbled as usual, but he knew the choice was right; next to Langer he was the strongest. Without comment they gave Manny's gear to Yuri. He picked what would be needed; the rest would be left in the tank.

· "Okay, Yuri take the lead and break ground for us. We'll switch off every fifteen minutes on the point. Move out!"

Yuri, Teacher, Gus, with Langer bringing up the drag, moved deeper into the trees, each following in the steps of the other.

Overhead the eagles of the war flew high, aloof in the clean crisp air of the sky. They flew far above the insects below, killing from the heights, never seeing the faces of their victims and seldom those of their own dead. The engines droned, who they were didn't matter, the men sweating their way through the crusty snow were alone, for now.

With the dark silence, came only the whispering of the wind, as it skimmed over the trees. Night, the kind that comes only to the cold lands, dark yet luminous. The trees, giant silent sentinels, unconcerned with the ambitions of man. Only the labored breathing of those beneath their branches disturbed the primeval serenity of this winter picture.

Before midnight, Langer called a halt. They had put enough distance between them and their stranded tank to feel safe enough to make camp. Doubling up, each joined his shelter half to that of another, strung them up between trees and piled snow up on the side to help keep the warmth in and the wind out. Gus was with Yuri, and Teacher and Langer shared the other. Inside the small havens they laid tree branches from the firs and pines to keep them off the snow floor, pulled themselves inside, and buttoned up the entrance. There would be no sentries tonight. They were too tired, far from the battle lines, and deep in the woods; it would be highly unlikely that any Russian patrol would find this one small spot before dawn.

Teacher pulled his knees up to his chest, putting his gloved hands under his armpits, hugging himself to get any extra iota of warmth. It was completely black inside; only the feel of Langer's body next to him and the man's breathing told of another presence.

"Carl, what the hell are you?"

Langer shifted, paused, and replied in a low, gentle voice that Teacher had seldom heard, "A man, nothing more. Perhaps even less."

A deep sighing exhalation told Teacher that Langer was asleep. And that was all the answer he was going to get. Nothing more, maybe less, what kind of damned answer is that? He, too, used the soldier's trick of taking a deep breath and letting it out slowly. Before the exhalation was completed he was asleep, the dull sleep of bone-weary fatigue that takes the soul and pulls one down into the darkness that heals.

Morning came with a light breeze whipping the flaps of the shelter halves gently, making soft flopping noises. The men crawled out of the shelters like winter bears shaking their bodies and heads to get rid of the sleep still hanging on them. One small smokeless fire for their rations and ersatz coffee. Gus complained it tasted like camel piss, and Langer thanked him for the information, saying that he had always wondered what camel piss tasted like, and now thanks to Gus's previous experiences, he knew.

Three days through the forest. Stumbling, cold, dragging, days before they reached the other side. Not once had they seen a sign of man or any large animals. Not the track of a single deer; only the small prints of squirrels and rabbits marked the purity of the winter covering. In three days they covered twenty kilometers. Only a hundred and seventy-five to go . . . on empty stomachs.

Two more days found them in a great open plain with no shelter other than what they could make from their own gear. Before noon of the following day they saw waves of bombers at about 15,000 heading west. Fifteen minutes later they saw them coming back. Barely visible in the distance was a black haze rising. . . .

"Novy Bug. We must still have people holding out there." Teacher barely nodded; it took too much effort to reply.

Langer called back to Yuri, who looked in the direction of the smoke, following Langer's pointing finger. "You've got the best eyes here, Yuri. How far?"

Yuri looked straight at the smoke then from the sides of his eyes. "Two more days the way we move now, perhaps twenty kilometers, no more."

Langer hiked his pack up a little higher, easing the straps. "All right. Let's go and take a look."

That night there would be no fires. They could hear the crumping of artillery pieces being fired; 105s and 155s. Ivan was in front of them.

That same night Langer climbed a small hillock and stood, eyes to the west, watching the flickering lights from the Russian guns, marking them in his mind. About forty-six kilometers; at their rate of march it would take them seven or eight hours to reach them and the German lines were beyond them another fifteen or so. He thought hard, trying to analyze the options.

His face was rough from an ice-crusted beard; frost spots on his cheeks gave them a higher look accenting the deep hollows of the eyes. *We've got to have food. Another day and night without any and Teacher and Gus won't make it. Yuri can but he's not as civilized as they are. He could last another three or four days just by eating the leather from his boots.*

He gave his head one quick jerk up and down. A decision was made. Twelve hours till dawn; if they moved now they could reach the Russian positions well before daylight. Rousting the others out he told them what was going to happen.

The Russians had food and they were going to get it tonight. Gus perked up at the idea of eating. His stomach had been trying to digest itself for the last two days and while the sounds Gus made while feeding normally were disgusting enough, the constant whining and gurgling of his gut was worse.

Indian file, as usual, they worked and labored their way through the drifts, every step taking them closer to either food or death, but either one was acceptable at this point. At least they were doing something positive, not waiting for the cold or starvation and exhaustion to take them one by one. Yuri, while able to go further than the others on an empty stomach, thought he caught a hungry look in Gus's eyes a time or two when the neanderthal had been watching him. Yuri had no doubt that before Gus succumbed to hunger he would indulge himself in a little stringy Tatar stew and there was only one Tatar in sight, HIM. He was ready to go, too.

The idea of Gus gnawing on his bones gave him a new incentive to reach the Russian lines, and he volunteered to break trail knowing he would take the best and fastest route to an alternate food source.

It wasn't difficult to locate the Russian guns; all they had to do was head toward the sounds of firing. Lying on their bellies they watched the Russian HQ, just behind the battery of four 105s. It was quiet. Ivan was careless or overconfident; they had no sentries to their rear. After all, they knew all the Germans were bottled up in Novy Bug. Yuri slid on his belly, soundlessly. He took advantage of every dip and drift to ease himself closer to the entrance of the peasants hut serving as a command post for the battery commander. Close behind came Langer. Gus and Teacher took the flanks to provide cover in case any more Russians showed up before they finished their business inside.

The battery was continuing to fire regularly spaced shots in sequence, first one then another on rotation, a steady, continuous, methodical order, designed to get the most out of their weapons and give each one's barrel some cooling time and thereby prolong the life of the guns. It would also serve to muffle any sounds that might come from the interior of the hut.

Yuri reached the side of the hut and crept on hands and knees to the edge of the doorway. Standing on the right he drew his butcher knife and held it low to his side, sharp edge up. Langer moved to the other side, preferring the long-bladed bayonet from a Mauser. He had honed down both sides to razor fineness. They listened to the beat of their hearts pounding like drums in their ears. A shaft of reddish gold light glowed weakly through a crack in the door. Putting his eye against it Carl tried to take in as much of the room as possible.

Three men were visible, two lying on pallets and one sitting at a Russian field desk, going over charts, probably working out the coordinates for the morning's firing program. From his shoulder boards it seemed he was a lieutenant. Tapping at the door softly, so as not to wake the sleeping men, Langer gave a strange whisper, *Tovarisch! Idisodar charoscho!* The lieutenant raised his head, *Shto?* Langer repeated his message to come in a hurry.

Sighing, the officer raised himself heavily from his seat and took the four steps to the door. Raising the wooden latch he opened the door and stepped out, only to find a hand gripping his throat, twisting his body around, cutting off his breath. The next thing he felt was a deep burning; Yuri's butcher knife found its way unerringly into the man's heart, severing the aorta. Langer let the body down easy.

Blades held low to the front in a half crouch, they stepped inside.

They moved swiftly inside, blades ready. The source of light was from a field lantern sitting on a couple of wooden shell crates for the howitzers. Yuri moved to the side of one of the sleeping Russians. Langer picked the other, a sergeant from the markings of his shoulder boards. Langer gave a quick nod of his head and both men moved, covering the mouths of their victims as the blades struck deep.

Langer and Yuri quickly looted the hut of all they could carry that would be of any use to them, mainly food and a couple of bottles of vodka. These they stuffed into one of the Russian field packs lying on the dirt floor. They moved back out into the dark, taking the same route away from the hut.

Gus and Teacher had been lying on their bellies, waiting. The cold of the ice crust creeping up through their uniforms was starting to stiffen them, making them sluggish, and slow to respond. Langer had to call twice before Teacher answered. Grabbing him by the shoulders he pulled him to his feet as Gus slowly rose from his icy bed.

Yuri cracked one of the bottles of vodka and stuck it in Gus's paw. Two quick swallows and half the bottle was gone down Gus's gaping gap-toothed maw. Reluctantly he handed the bottle back to Yuri, who passed it over to Teacher. A couple of gulps and Teacher, too, felt some renewed strength and warmth.

There was no need to ask what had happened in the hut. The fact that they had returned spoke for itself.

Wraithlike, they moved away from the guns. Circling wide, they tried to get as much distance between themselves and the hut as possible before the Russians' bodies were discovered by their comrades. If they were lucky the Ivans would think the killers had come from Novy Bug, a reconnaissance patrol that stumbled on the hut and now were back in their own lines.

That morning there was no breaking of the dawn, just a gradual lightening of the sky to dull grey. Another storm was coming. The four sat huddled in a snow cave, lying on their shelter halves and blankets, of which each had one. This helped to keep the cold from the floor of their makeshift shelter to a bearable level. They fed on coarse black Russian bread and goat cheese. Gus was bitching because Langer wouldn't let them finish off the last bottle of vodka. But Langer knew that a couple of drinks were okay, but too much alcohol in the system actually lowered the body temperature, even though you felt warmer for taking another drink. They needed to reserve all the body heat they could, if the storm blasting over the Ukrainian plains was to leave them alive at its end. This night the winds were fifty KPH and growing in intensity. Here, huddled together, they had to wait and let the storm use up its strength while they tried to conserve theirs.

Sleep, the great healer, was their best ally, and they used him as much as they could, letting the darkness take them for hours at a time. They woke only to repair an item of their gear, or to eat a piece of bread. They filled their canteens with snow from outside and waited for it to melt, then drank and slept some more. They only left their cave to take a leak or crap and scurried back to their burrow cursing. The storm passed, leaving a startling clearness. The new snow sparkled with millions of flashing diamonds, each one a pinprick to the light-sensitive eyes of the cave dwellers. A brilliant crystal cold day, the air bit at their lungs and skin.

CHAPTER THIRTEEN

At the Ingul they crossed over what in the spring would be swift flow, now frozen solid to a depth of five feet. An eighty-ton tank could rumble over it with no fear of crashing through.

They decided not to try and break through the Russian lines to their own forces at Novy Bug. With the food they had picked up at the hut they had a better chance of making it on to their original destination at Yuzhney Bug. Twelve days of crisp clear weather and they reached the first German outposts. Staggering in they almost had their asses shot off by the machine-gun crew sitting behind an MG-42. Only Gus's string of curses which could have been heard clear to Berlin stopped the gun crew from ripping them to pieces.

Ragged, bearded, filthy caricatures of soldiers, they were hustled to the rear in an amphibious Volkswagen. They were shown into the presence of

117

an immaculate colonel of Jagers, a man who obviously considered those beneath him fit only to do his bidding.

Langer read the martinet correctly and reported in the best military manner. "Sir, *Stabsfeldwebel* Carl Langer begs to report that he has reported back to German forces with three other ranks following the destruction of our tank in the battle around Nikopol three weeks ago."

Colonel von Mancken rose from behind his field desk and stepped in front of Langer, looking the man up and down in distaste. Wrinkling his nose at the odor of this disgrace to the glory of German arms, he said, "You mean you came all the way from Nikopol? I do hope you have a proper explanation or I assure you that you and those with you will most certainly face a court martial for desertion." He called for his regimental sergeant major, a huge Bavarian with a barrel chest. He had the look of a man who enjoys the power he has over others.

"*Stabswachtmeister* Schmitt, have these men issued new uniforms and cleaned up. You will report of their activities since they left their unit at Nikopol. You will report back to me at fifteen hundred hours with the report and these men."

Schmitt clicked his heels together. "*Zum Befehl*, Herr Oberst." Turning his attention to Langer he barked out as if he were on a drill field, "*Achtung*, about face, quick march. *Eins, zwei, drei, vier*," He literally tried to goose-step Langer out of the door.

Once out into the open, leaving the colonel to his delusions of grandeur in his log and sandbag HQ, he halted Langer. "Okay, knock off the tin soldier shit. You're in a lot of trouble. That prissy bastard in there will have you before a firing squad in the morning unless you have some help. Do you have anything to trade for the services I might be able to render you in the name of German soldiery? Gold, silver, jewels, opium. I'm not hard to get along with; almost anything will do that I can resell."

Teacher and the others joined Langer, who had had just about enough. He looked the sergeant major over carefully. The lack of combat badges or ribbons was obvious. This was one of those bullies who had spent the last four years in some training regiment, impressing recruits and being careful to make themselves indispensable to their commanders in order to avoid going to the front. But time had caught up with this one and he was on the front, now. It was high time he learned a reality.

Gus moved up closer to Schmitt; Yuri began to give his butcher knife a finer edge, stropping it on his boot tops, while squinting and looking up at Schmitt, grinning. His gold tooth gleamed in a dark, wizened face. Teacher merely smiled and began fondling his submachine gun. Schmitt hesitated. What was this? Why weren't they afraid of him? He was a sergeant major and outranked them. Everyone had always been afraid of him back in Germany.

Langer moved up closer to Schmitt, his face only inches away from the other's. "Listen to me. I have seen your type for years and you're a gutless piece of suet. You can get away with that bullshit back in Germany, but here on the front it's a little bit different. You mess with us and I'll twist your head off your shoulders. Do you know what it means to die? For your sake I hope so. Now get away from me and go scare some children."

The first real fear he had ever known struck him. Schmitt took a step back in shock. He had been on the front only two weeks, and there had not even been a shot fired other than an occasional sniper and that was on the lines, a place he carefully avoided. He cursed himself. His mistake was making himself too indispensable to Col. von Mancken. When the colonel received orders to the front he just had to take his faithful sergeant major with him. The pompous bastard! Blustering, he tried to fake it. "You watch your step. I'm the boss here and you heard what the colonel said. The showers are over behind supply. Get cleaned up and write out your report. I'll see you later."

Langer snorted and turned his back on him. Yuri rose from his squatting position and passed in front of Schmitt. Smiling and bobbing his head, he took out a small bulging cloth bag. He grinned as he pressed it into Schmitt's hands. "For Germanski, presento." Gold tooth gleaming he followed after the others.

Schmitt, who was used to his lessers presenting him with tokens of their esteem, mumbled to himself that the savage had more sense and manners than the others. At least he recognized his betters. "Wonder what it is?" Pulling the drawstring open, he shook the contents out into his hand and froze; his gut squirmed and he let the contents fall to lie on the snow. Ears! Human ears! A dozen or more, all from the right side. Sweat broke out on his forehead in spite of the cold. He backed away and almost ran back into the security of headquarters.

The showers were a canvas field tent with empty petrol drums set up outside filled with water. It had a stovepipe affair running from an old wood-burning stove, up through the center of the drums to heat the water. Crude, but right now it was the most luxurious innovation they had ever experienced. All except Yuri, who distrusted water in any form other than drinking, but he gave in to the demands of the others that shed his lice-infested rags and joined in.

Gus, removing his boots, let out a yelp of pure joy. "Here, fellows, look what I got." He had to peel his socks off and there exposed to daylight for the first time in days were two blackened toes on his left foot, the two small ones, black and dead; frostbite. "I got my bleeding ticket out of here, ain't they beautiful?"

Gus refused to go to the dispensary until after he washed. "There's no rush, they ain't goin' no place, for a while, that is." A supply clerk came over with clean uniforms for them after they had been deloused. The only one who wasn't infested was Langer. For some reason the little bastards didn't like the taste of him, but the others had to submit to a complete spraying and laughed as their clothes were tossed into the wood stove. They enjoyed each hissing pop that said another Russian louse was cremated. Of those they had inspected only a few had the little gray cross on them that said they were the carriers of typhus. In the early days of the war you could get a couple of marks apiece for each of

them you turned in to the medics for shipment back
to Germany, where they were analyzed and tested.
By now there were probably more of them in the
Fatherland than in Russia.

Gus joyfully presented himself to regimental hospital. An hour later the doctor took a pair of pliers
and simply pulled the two blackened toes off without the benefit of any anesthetic. Taking a pair of
surgical scissors he trimmed up the edges, rinsed off
the foot with a little raw alcohol, sprinkled it with
sulfa powder and cursed him all the time for being
a slackard and a defeatist. That there was no good
reason for anyone to get frostbite if they only took
proper care of themselves. It was treason not to take
proper maintenance of an item that was the property of the state, even a piece of obviously defective
equipment as the traitorous *Stabsgefreiter* clearly
was. Gus asked the doctor how he'd like to have
his ass stuck in a snow bank for three weeks and
then see how much would be left after the
Stabsgefreiter, by the grace of our Holy German or
Austrian Führer, took a pair of his pliers to it.

After Gus proceeded to describe what he could
do with his pliers to other portions of the doctor's
anatomy, he was hurriedly moved out to a hospital
ward. The doctor made a note to have the man's
mental condition tested. He was most certainly, at
the least, a nonsocial and emotionally disturbed
person who shouldn't be permitted to run around
loose without professional supervision. At fifteen
hundred hours Langer, Teacher and Yuri presented
themselves to the sergeant major at regimental HQ.
The clean uniforms and showers gave them a

semblance of military appearance. The Knight's Cross around Langer's neck did more than anything else to give Schmitt a case of the jitters. You didn't get one of those for kissing babies. Taking their paybooks and papers, Schmitt knocked on the colonel's door and received permission to enter.

Returning, he told them to stand easy and wait. It would be a while; the colonel was busy. Ten minutes later a *Blitzmädel* left the colonel's office, looking pleased with herself. She took a look at the Knight's Cross holder and the man's rugged face and smiled, wet her lips, patted back her light brown hair done in an efficient bun, and exited after one more smile.

Schmitt knocked on the door and received permission to send Langer and the others in.

When they presented themselves, Yuri stayed slightly to the rear. He had never liked officers of any kind. Russian or German made no difference, they only meant one thing to him: trouble.

Colonel von Mancken peered at Langer and then Teacher. Pointing a manicured finger at Yuri, he inquired, "What, may I ask, is that?"

"A volunteer, sir, one who has fought well for us," he added. Von Mancken raised an eyebrow. "I did not ask for a list of his merits, Sergeant. I asked what is he?"

"A Tatar, Sir."

Von Mancken viewed the Asiatic with distaste, shaking his head. "What is the Reich coming to when it uses the likes of a patently subhuman type to fight battles that should be won by the glorious feats of arms of Germany's Aryan youth? Indeed a sad state of affairs." He dismissed the Tatar from his mind as he would have a dog or any beast.

"Sergeant Langer, I have made some inquiries." He held Langer's and the others' paybooks and papers in front of him. A trace of envy touched him when he eyed the Knight's Cross and he promised himself to get one before much longer, and one with the oak leaves to it. It would certainly add greatly to his career.

"I have communicated with the commander of your former division and he referred me to the headquarters of Field Marshal von Manstein, who it appears awarded your decoration. It is his desire that you and your companions be given transport to a rest area. That includes your savage also."

The colonel omitted the fact that he had been informed by the field marshal's aide de camp that the Herr Field Marshal did not like for anyone to cast doubts on the valor of anyone he had personally decorated, especially when such a person had been not in combat himself. It would most certainly not be pleasing to the Herr Field Marshal and could have unhappy results for anyone so shortsighted as to commit such an offense. Did the Herr Colonel understand? Or was he addressing a major? Ranks changed so rapidly at the front it was often quite difficult to keep track of all the demotions, they happened so rapidly.

Von Mancken returned his attention to the men in front of him. He was careful to keep control; one must not give vent to displays of emotion in front of the enlisted men. "It will take a few days for orders to be prepared. Until that time you will have no duties here; just don't start any trouble. Schmitt will see to your quarter assignments. You're dismissed."

Langer and Teacher clicked heels, saluted and left followed by a scowling Yuri. The Tatar could smell the envy and hate in the colonel. Well, maybe he would have to start a new collection of ears.

For Langer and his men, the next days were ones like they had not known for years. All the food they could eat and more. Gus ate like a barbarian king. His threats against the medical orderlies' private parts kept them in a state of constant fear and attendance. He gorged on sausage and cabbage, swilling it down with huge amounts of whatever was to be had, from Czech beer to medical alcohol cut with water and flavored with just a touch of iodine. He swore it tasted exactly like good Scotch whiskey.

Every time Yuri saw *Stabswachtmeister* Schmitt he would just smile and tug at his ear lobe. Schmitt kept as much space between himself and the little brown man from the steppes as possible.

The New Year was celebrated by a small party. The *Blitzmädel* decided to try the scar-faced tanker on for size. When they left the privacy of the storeroom they had used for their meeting, she could barely walk. Never had she experienced anything like that night. The Panzerman had put her through movements that she had only seen in school when they had studied the art of India. And she had snuck a forbidden look at a copy of the Kama Sutra one of her classmates had ordered

125

from a pornography house in Bremen. The sergeant could have, in her opinion, written the damned thing.

Gus had managed to acquire enough chits for a visit to a field whorehouse a few kilometers to the rear by cheating the orderlies at cards, dice or anything else he could force them into betting on. The fact that they knew he was cheating was of no consequence. He wouldn't take no for an answer and when he, as he said, had to gently shake one of them, a two-hundred-and-fifty-pound supply sergeant, the rest decided it would be wiser not to irritate the madman any more than necessary. The supply sergeant was now in traction.

CHAPTER FOURTEEN

Yuri never got his wish to begin a new ear collection. Langer received his transit orders and they were moved out to a training regiment at Vilnyus in Lithuania. Two days after they arrived, Hitler relieved von Manstein of command of the sector they had just left and replaced him with Field Marshal Model, the one they called The Fireman. The wiry, thin-faced field marshal was known for his brilliance in handling crisis situations, and had time and again foiled Russian plans to annihilate German forces they had bottled up. Model was a master of fighting withdrawals, stretching the pursuing enemy out to the limits of supply and knowing just when to turn and fight.

For the most part German forces tried to straighten their lines and set up barriers to slow down the Russian winter offensive. Leningrad finally had to be evacuated after three years of siege.

The Russians still managed to advance to the Bug and Dniester rivers despite brilliant counterattacks by Manstein. The trapped 1st Panzer Army at Tarnopol managed to fight its way out almost intact with the aid of the Luftwaffe, which air dropped all of its supplies. The old reliable Junker 52 workhorse tri-motor was the back bone of a massive air resupply. Langer and Teacher spent the remainder of the winter trying to cram as much training as they could onto the replacements being sent up. It was woefully short many times. The boys they sent up had less than ten days' familiarization with their weapons. Gus was disappointed in his hopes to be sent back and discharged. Instead he was returned to Langer in May, busted down to private. Ivan had a habit of treating prisoners according to their rank; the higher you were, the worse they gave you. A private could always claim he was forced into the war and was really a Communist at heart.

The spring campaigns opened when the ground was firm enough to handle the weight of the armored vehicles. Langer wasn't worried about going up to the front. He knew that the front would soon come to them. It was just a matter of time. In the meantime, he did the best he could to teach the replacements how to survive, not that it did much good. Already, most of the replacements were no more than seventeen, but the Russians, too, were showing some of the strain of replacing troops. They had lost millions and were now fleshing out their ranks with boys of fifteen and old men of sixty. Anyone capable of carrying a weapon was called

into service. There was no medical excuse that
could save one from the army, unless he was an am-
putee or cripple.

On 6 March, Colonel von Mancken did his best
to win the Knight's Cross and was promptly ground
into jelly by the tracks of one of the new JS-I
(Joseph Stalin) heavy tanks. *Stabswachmeister*
Schmitt managed to steal the colonel's car and drive
fifteen kilometers to the rear, where he tried to
bribe a couple of hard-nosed members of the field
gendarmerie, who promptly hung him by the neck
from a telegraph pole and divided up his bribe
among themselves anyway.

By mid-April the Russians had advanced to striking range of the frontier of Poland and were facing
the Carpathian mountains to the south. The Crimea
had fallen, the 17th Army fought without support
until it could hold out no longer. Some units were
rescued in a German version of Dunkirk but not all.
Thousands of horses were driven off the cliffs to
drown in the Black Sea, the German defenders' last
act. Destroy anything that might be of use to the
Russians. By the end of July Langer's prediction
that the front would come to them came true. They
were pushed out of Vilnyus to form a hedgehog
northwest of the city, surrounded and cut off.

Yuri motioned to Gus to come and take a look.
Gus raised his head up far enough to get a good look
at a T-34 sitting just a block away beside a burned-
out bakery on the outskirts of Vilnyus. The crew was

taking a break to enjoy their lunch. They had already strung up, and were butchering a pig for their lunch.

Gus whispered to Langer, who was talking to Teacher. "Hey Sarge, chow time. There's only four of them."

Langer took a look, not at the pig, but the tank. "You're right, Gus, and there's our way out of here."

Gus looked at the sitting T-34 and smiled. "I'll make you a deal. You get the tank and I'll get the pig."

"Good enough, but let's keep it quiet; no shooting unless we have to. Let's not let their cousins know we're here if we can help it. Teacher, you take the Mauser and cover us. Yuri, you come at them from around the rear of the bakery and wait until Gus and I move before you hit them. Gus and I will handle the three with the pig. You take out the one by the tank. Got it?" Yuri grinned his sparkling gold smile.

"All right, then let's be at it."

Gus took his entrenching tool from its case. He had, as usual, honed the edge down fine enough to cut silk with. Yuri had his butcher knife and Langer the long M-98 bayonet. They didn't have much doubt that they would be able to get close enough to use their blades. The Ivans were totally involved with gutting the pig and building a cook fire.

Bellies to the ground, they slid out through the brush and grass slithering like snakes. Before Vilnyus had fallen they had been issued new uniforms and the summer camouflage of light and dark brown splinter patterns blended beautifully with the cover they used.

They moved slowly, the smell of the grass in their nostrils. The heat of the sun beat down their backs and small rivers of sweat ran down the hollow of their spines.

Teacher watched from the cellar window. It seemed to take forever for them to cover the short distance to the bakery wall. Langer raised his head for a quick look.

One of the Ivans was showing off to the others, making swipes with a saber through the air, obviously showing them how it was done when he was still in the mounted calvary. Langer focused on him. That could be dangerous. The swordsman wore the collar tabs of a major. He looked to be about thirty-five. Lean, with high Slavic cheekbones and deep-set eyes that were always in a shadow. He moved through some quick ghost parrying-and-lunging techniques to the delight of his comrades, and with a whirling sweep severed the head from the pig.

Langer grunted mentally. Not bad. It's hard to cut through a neck like that, especially one as thick as a pig's. You have to hit at just the right spot between the vertebra or you can't do it. But it still takes a lot of strength just to cut through the muscle. The Order of Suvarov and the badge of a Hero of the Soviet Union were easily visible.

They reached the wall, their hearts pounding but with the calmness that comes before action. Yuri moved around the building, keeping close to the wall. He had until the time it took him to count his fingers and toes twice slowly, then Langer and Gus would move.

Gus pointed out one of the Ivans. A big man almost as large as himself, bending over slicing up the pig's hindquarters. Whispering, "That's my meat."

Langer nodded he'd take out the major first, and then the little Armenian-looking one by the tank would go to whoever was closest. Yuri would get the one closest to him, a youngster who looked more German than Russian, probably from the Caucasus.

It was time. Langer touched Gus on the shoulder and nodded, took a deep breath, and moved straight at the major. Gus followed, his entrenching tool held like a barbarian axe from the days of the Vikings.

Gus lurched out in front of Langer, the entrenching tool above his head, aiming to slice through the neck of the big Russian who was involved in pulling the intestines out of the slaughtered pig. He was almost on him when his feet hit a slick pile of pig guts, and he went ass over end in a heap under the knife of the big Slav.

Langer rushed in behind before the Slav could react and slice up the new piece of bacon lying helpless at his feet. He yelled, the Slav turned, a slightly surprised look on his face; what had happened hadn't really registered. The look of blankness stayed there until Langer's bayonet made a whisshing sound and gave the big man another mouth, gaping and spouting.

Yuri came out at the same time, his butcher knife held low; he raced at half crouch up to the young boy, and whipped him around by the shoulder, aiming for the gut. The youngster twisted as Yuri struck, and the blade slid between the ribs on his left side. The point of the knife reached the heart, but the spasms of muscles, combined with the natural adhesion of the rib cage, made it impossible for Yuri to draw the blade back out. He set a foot on the youngster's head to hold him and began frantically to twist the blade, trying to break it free, only to feel it snap at the handle. Spinning around, he had just enough time to see the look of pleasure on the Cossack's face, before the saber half-severed his head from the body at the neck. Another flick of the wrist and the saber flashed again; the head fell to the ground before the body knew it was dead. Yuri's head fell to rest beside the tracks of the T-34, the face looking up, eyes open, the mouth wide in his familiar gold-toothed smile.

The Armenian was shocked at first, then started to scramble up the side of the tank to get inside and batten down. He had rolled out from under Langer, and out of the pig guts, some still hanging to his face and chest. Growling, Gus struck at him with the edge of his shovel. There was a "thunk," then a wet sucking sound, as it pulled out of the Armenian's spine. Gus had hit him right at the junction between the shoulder blades with a straight thrust that sank the sharpened sides in to a depth of five inches. Gus caught a look at Yuri's head lying on the ground by the tracks, and screamed like a berserker of old. He lunged forward, swinging his tool like a meat cleaver, only to feel his hand go numb, and find he was holding only the wooden handle. The head of the entrenching tool had been severed with a clean quarter wrist sweep of the major's saber hand.

The Cossack paused, noting that the Germans were carrying no guns; he decided to enjoy himself a little. He fended off Gus's attempt to brain him with the shovel handle with a series of light taps and touches, leaving the big German's face pricked and cut in half a dozen places, in less than ten seconds. Gus couldn't get through the flashing blade, and backed away, a wounded animal, his eyes shrunk to tiny pinpoints, blood running freely down his face. The major moved in the classic *flèche*, the long, smooth, almost running lunge to the heart; Gus was backed up to the tank with nowhere to run. The saber blade moved off center to ring off the hull of the T-34. The Cossack recovered.

Langer stood between them, his bayonet held to the front. The major smiled and spoke in perfect German, with a slightly British accent, "Well, well, what have we here, a sergeant who thinks he understands the saber. Too bad you're not an officer at least, then I might have the confidence that you would have at least had some rudimentary training. But perhaps you can provide me with enough entertainment to make up for the loss of my men." He looked closely at the thick-set body of the man confronting him. "You are a tough-looking swine at any rate." He pointed the saber blade at Langer's face, at the scarred side. "*Schlager mensur*, perhaps?" his voice hopeful as he referred to the German dueling scar students of the universities loved to inflict on each other as badges of courage. "Perhaps you have had some experience after all."

The Cossack stepped, made a mock *enveloppe-ment* that ended in the *en garde* position and saluted the man with the bayonet. "Sergei Ilye Rasdonovich at your service." Gus started to move, but Langer called out, loud enough for Teacher to hear, "Leave him alone. He's mine." The major thought he was only addressing Gus.

Teacher removed the Mauser from his shoulder and moved to a position where he could get a better look at the proceedings. He had seen Langer with a bayonet on a rifle or, in hand to hand, but this was different, a bayonet against a saber. He consoled himself with the thought that if Langer was killed, at least he would have the pleasure of putting a bullet through the brain of the Russian major.

Langer watched the body of the Russian; he was good, but he held his blade a little too tight, the arm was stiff and he was over confident. Carl held his blade with the cutting edge facing out to the right, the blade held flat, extended. He waited, went into a half crouch, right foot extended, his left hand held low to his side, fingers open. The Cossack finished his salute and extended the point of his saber, making a circular parry, small circles around the point of Langer's weapon, feeling the distance, and then performed a glide, not really wanting to kill, just toy with his mouse for a moment. The glide ended up being turned back on itself. The Cossack flinched.

His sleeve was opened from the wrist to the elbow, nothing deep, just enough to irritate, but how had the mouse done it? Pivoting, he again

faced the German; this time there would be no
toying with his prey, it was time to kill. He went on
to *coupe*, trying to pass his blade over the point of
the German's shorter bayonet by raising his point
with a flexible movement of the fingers and hand
bending the arm just a hair and extending to pierce
the heart. Again he felt a burning, as his blade was
turned and somehow his victim had come under
him and made a quick slice on the face in the same
spot that the German wore his scar. The Hun
stepped back and smiled, raised his blade in a
straight-arm salute, mocking him. "*Ave! te moritu
salutus.*" The ancient salute of the Roman arena.
Blood dripped down the Cossack's arm on to his
hand and wrist, making the grip slippery to the
touch. He bled just enough to fog the vision in his
left eye slightly. The Fascist was playing with him.
He was the mouse, and the smiling, blue-eyed man
in the strange stance in front of him was the cat.

Well, this mouse could still kill; with a cry he
lunged, making one circular sweeping attack after
another, trying to use the longer reach of his weapon to beat the German back and break through his
defense, only to find the German holding him chest
to chest for a moment, moving around like they
were dancing. The German smiled and
Rasdonovich again felt a stinging pain; this time the
German stepped back and laughed. Sergei touched
his face; the German had slit his nose an inch on
both sides, leaving only two bloody flaps to breathe
through.

Langer stepped back; the Cossack was breathing
heavily, bloody bubbles swelling out of the torn

nostrils and bursting with each breath. He knew he was going to die; he waited, Langer moved in, low blade extended. He lunged, the Cossack tried to parry. Langer's left hand grabbed the Russian's wrist, pulling him forward off balance; he then moved and stepped to the side, putting the arch of his boot on the back of Sergei's knee, forcing him down to the ground on one knee, sword arm held in a steel grip; another quick burning and Sergei saw his left ear lying in front of the Tatar's head.

Raising his head he cried out, "End it, in the name of God end it."

Langer smiled, his face like granite flesh. "As you wish." One long circular stroke like that of a master barber, a strong tug on the hair, and the Russian's head joined that of Yuri, the two of them watching each other.

Carl wiped his blade off on the Russian's tunic, and then resheathed it in its metal scabbard. It was over, and once more the old feeling of being drained washed over him.

Teacher came out of the cellar and joined Gus, speechless. He had never seen anything like the way Langer had played with the Cossack, breaking the man's spirit down before killing him. The Cossack never had a chance, he might as well have been unarmed. The positions and techniques used by Langer were not those taught in the fencing schools of Europe, at least not in this century. They resembled some of the old frescoes he had seen of gladiators in the Roman arena, right down to the Roman salute.

Langer stopped him before he could make any

comment. "All right, let's take care of the bodies. We don't want them found until later. We'll haul them over to the side of the bakery, there's a small ditch, we'll bury them there."

Gus pointed at Yuri. "What about him?"

"Him, too, but we'll bury him the way he would have liked, as chieftain of the high steppes."

Gus wondered what the hell that meant, but didn't really give a damn, his mind already on the fresh pork. The dead, it does no good to feel any more for them. Their troubles were over, and right now he was still hungry.

Teacher had a suspicion of what Langer meant, but kept his own council. Gus found out what his sergeant meant when Carl laid the dead Russians at the feet of the Tatar, placing Yuri's head where it belonged on his shoulders, his butcher knife in his hand. He held the Cossack's head in his own hands, grasping it to his chest. Langer backed away after they had filled the ditch, and faced the four corners of the world all the time making a slow, upward sweeping motion of his hand and chanting low beneath his breath. Gus knew he was watching some kind of religious ceremony, but just what, he couldn't fathom.

"What is he doing, Teacher? You know everything, all those books you read."

Responding, in a low voice in order not to interrupt the proceedings, he explained as best he could, for Gus's simple mind.

The ceremony completed, Langer looked at the wondering faces of Gus and Teacher. "I'll tell you about it later. Right now let's get loaded and haul ass out of here."

Once in the T-34, Gus took a moment to familiarize himself with the controls. "It's just like a tractor, Sarge; no problem."

"Teacher, you take the hull gun, I'll handle the turret and 76 mm."

Gus squealed with pleasure. "Look here, Sarge." He held up one of the new Russian PPs 43 submachine guns and a bottle of vodka. "We're loaded for bear now." He cracked open the bottle and drained it. The pig's carcass rested right behind the driver's seat, close to him. He wasn't going to let anything happen to his dinner. If they had to bail out of the tank, it was even odds which he would take, the submachine gun or the pig. Langer gave odds mentally on the pig.

CHAPTER FIFTEEN

They spent the rest of the day in a wrecked barn, moving the tank straight through the side. They had been bypassed in the night; the rest of the German forces in the pocket were an hour's march to the west. Most of them would never make it to the new line outside Kaunas. Langer would wait for dark and move through the Russian lines right down the rail tracks after bypassing the German pocket of resistance. Once past that, they should have easy going until they reached the bridge at Nieman. They would have to be careful or the defenders, thinking they were Russians, would blow them away.

That night they fed on roast pig. Gus, gulping down chunks of half-raw meat and swigging vodka, reminded Langer of someone he had known long ago in another place.

The fuel gauges showed half a tank of gas, more

than enough to reach the bridge crossing at Kaunas. On good roads the T-34 had a range of over 250 kilometers. At dusk they moved out, the clanking of the treads a familiar, friendly sound. As they swung through the fields, Carl put on a Russian tanker's leather helmet, put his head out of the turret and called out directions. They passed burned-out villages and hamlets, isolated farms and houses, which had all received the same treatment. This was the first of the enemy countries that had fallen to the Soviets. Twice, Langer had to forcibly restrain Gus when they passed a couple of farmhouses and saw the women of the farm nailed to the barn doors, their men and children lying in front of them. The women had obviously been raped. Gus wanted to head for the nearest Russian unit and run them down under the treads of their own tank.

The road leading to the frontiers of East Prussia were littered with burned-out transport and tanks; dead horses lay bloated all along the way, their legs stiff, the carts and guns they had been pulling turned over or burned and the contents looted. The bodies of men lay by the hundreds where Soviet armor had overrun the slower, horse-drawn wagons. Near them were neat, orderly ranks of men that had been lined up first and machine gunned down in rows.

The T-34 was passed by fast trucks filled with laughing Russians, the victors heading to the new line. They waved to their comrades in the tank and wished them well in continuing their slaughter. Langer himself had to force his mind elsewhere and resist the temptation to send a shell into them and blow the savages to pieces. Savages? What difference did it make who did the killing, they're no better or worse than the Nazis. The truth of the matter was, the Nazis were perhaps more horrible in that they were educated men who sometimes cried over something tragic in an opera, and then would order thousands of deaths in the concentration camps.

The Russians were brutal, but it was the mindless brutality of the hordes that had ravaged Europe centuries before. Fewer than one out of a hundred could write his own name, and fewer than that among those who came from Asian Russia. They were the ones most feared; they had the blood of the vanquished legions of Genghis Khan and the Huns in their veins and were now let loose on the world to do what their instincts told them they did best, kill.

Trucks were beginning to slow down; they were reaching the staging areas of the Soviets. Langer moved the tank off the road to the side and had to slow down carefully to avoid running over the milling infantry. He waved and laughed at jokes, and kept on going, ignoring offers to stop and drink, or eat. He called out orders and kept moving. To stop risked being found out and he had no desire to be sent to the slave camps in Siberia.

The flames of burning villages were small bright spots on the plains, the smell of smoke carried to them by a gentle northerly wind coming off the Baltic Sea. They were nearing the last Soviet positions as was evidenced by the freshly dug bunkers and position lines of cannon being pulled into position. The Russians believed in cannon just as Napoleon did; the more the better, and they had plenty more.

The German positions were marked by the impact of Russian rockets and artillery. The bridge still held. Continuous fire from concrete bunkers made it extremely hazardous for any Russian tank that tried to approach them. Already a half dozen lay on and off the tracks of the rail bridge, evidence of the German gunners' accuracy and tenacity. Russians waved the oncoming T-34 on, praising the courage of the crew riding into the face of almost certain death, *"Urra! Urra!"*

They had one hope of getting through; in front of them was a former German pillbox, now occupied by the elite guard troops of Marshal Chernyakhovsky. Leaping down to Gus and Teacher, Carl explained, "All right, this is it. I'm going to take out the bunker, you just get this bastard over the bridge and when you reach the center un-ass it."

"Teacher, you won't be needed on the MG when we stop. You bail out and toss a grenade in before you leave. That should blow this bastard to hell and let our guys know that we're on their side.

"Gus, you use that magnificent set of lungs to yell as loud as you can that we're Germans and coming through, and not to fire. Everybody got it?"

Teacher acknowledged the order and Gus fretted and bitched about his leftover pig and what to do with it.

The unsuspecting Russians in the bunker raised their fists and saluted. A round from a 75 mm pak whanged off the glass plating and ricocheted into the night. Langer swung the turret over slightly at a range of less than twenty meters and fired. The bunker erupted; the Russians died without ever knowing they had been tricked. On the German side, a lieutenant held his fire, confident that he had plenty of time to take out the lone tank; there was no rush, he had a good crew that had already destroyed over forty Russian tanks; the rings around the barrels of their guns kept an accurate count for them. *What's this!? The Russian has stopped dead in the center, the crew is getting out. Why?* He called to his infantry support to train their machine guns on the crewmen.

The T-34 exploded, a burned, twisted hulk was all that remained, all in less than thirty seconds. The gunners on the MG-42 sighted only a monstrous bellowing Gus, which halted the pulling of the triggers.

"Don't shoot, you sons of bitches, it's Gus Beiderman and a couple of friends back from the dead." He led the way, twisting and dodging all the time, keeping up his cursing order not to fire. One of the gunners was tempted anyway; he recognized the voice as belonging to a human gorilla who cheated him out of two months' pay shooting craps.

The Russians finally woke up and got around to sending round after round at the fleeing impostors. Tracers licked their heels and flashed between their legs. Gus yelped as one of them left the inside of his trousers singed, and burned his thigh just inches from the pride and hope of German womanhood.

* * *

From August on, they fought with one unit, then another, as the Russian advances continued, more slowly than in the spring, but still advancing a few more yards or kilometers every day as the supply lines of the Soviet forces built up their reserves for the push into Germany itself. The Russians held back their armies when the Polish Home Army revolted against the Nazis. Because the Poles were not Communists, Stalin held back his forces until the SS could eliminate them in fierce house-to-house battles that wiped out all effective non-Communist resistance that his forces might encounter.

By the end of August, Langer and his men were in East Prussia facing again their old nemesis from the great battles at Kursk and Kharkov. Here in East Prussia the German forces resisted with fanatical determination, but it was of no avail. There were too few men and weapons were left spread out over a front stretching 1,600 kilometers. General Busch's Army Group Center, which Langer had been attached to at Vilnyus, had been decimated. Twenty-five divisions had been trapped; only eight escaped. Most of the captured Germans were simply mowed down. They were the thousands of bodies they had passed on the tracks leading to Kaunas. The Russians claimed 158,000 captured and nearly 400,000 dead. By the time the leaves began to turn, Army Group North was trapped with its back to the Baltic. The Russians were content to leave them where they were tying up the German armies there, with minimal forces keeping them from breaking up to join Army Group Center to the south. They didn't know the situation or they would have attempted to break out. Anyway, Hitler had ordered them to remain there, tying up men that could have been used at the undermanned center.

By the end of October they were still holding the front on the borders of East Prussia. News from the west was scanty and filled with phrases from the minister of propaganda, such as fanatical promises of secret weapons to be unleashed on the allies.

Gus farted at this news. "Secret weapons, my ass; they can't even produce the old ones. I ain't seen a German fighter in the air for weeks. What the hell happened to them all?"

Teacher merely shook his head, "It's all just about over, I don't know why they don't just finish us off now, what the hell do we have left to fight with?"

Langer lit a smoke from a pack of Russian cigarets that he had taken off a body; they tasted dry and acrid in his mouth. "They aren't going to finish us off for a while, not with winter coming on and before that the rains slowing things down a bit before their supply lines can catch up to them. I'd guess it would be spring before the big push comes; they have time on their side. Step by step they push us back and shorten the lines a little. They're finally forcing us to do what should have been done years ago and concentrate our forces where we could get the most strength from them, not stretch them out all over the whole of Russia." Exhaling, he smelled the air. "No, it will go on a while longer."

The earth shook under them as a salvage of heavy Russian artillery ranged about them; the big guns were being brought up. The more familiar sounds of the 76 mm was superseded by the heavier crump of guns up to 210 mm firing a shell that weighed 297 pounds. One of these crater makers hit less than forty feet away, blowing Gus clear out of his fox-hole, landing him fifteen feet away, ears ringing and deaf. Langer raced out, grabbed him and dragged him back into a hole. For the next week Gus said he heard the bells of the cathedrals in Cologne, playing the "Horst Wessel Lied."

Gus finally disappeared in the middle of October while out scrounging for food; he just walked off to the rear of a village he was visiting between Suwalki and Johannesburg. He had heard that there was a supply depot there holding rations which they had received no orders to distribute. The Russians had picked that time to blast the village from the face of the earth with a barrage from their big guns, combined with an air strike of twin-engine bombers. The last Langer had seen of him was his waddling walk; he had picked up a new style of walking to compensate for the loss of his toes. It made him change the pressure of his step and gave him a gait that looked as if he was about to lose his balance and fall over on his already pushed-in face.

Langer and Teacher searched the rubble of the village and found only the dead. Supplies not destroyed were spread out over three miles and already the scavengers, soldiers and civilians, were fighting over tins of burned food. Of Gus, they assumed that he had finally gone to meet the great quartermaster in the sky, where the clouds rained

vodka and the women were always young and pretty. The two made their way alone, stopping to stay
awhile with one group, then another, until they
were rounded up by some field police in Allenstein
along with others and formed into a new group and
assigned orders to return to the front. They would
have to make their way on foot, there was no transportation available, but from this day on, anyone
without written orders would be shot or hung on
sight. They shrugged; what difference did it make,
now or later? At least it gave them something to do,
rather than just wait.

CHAPTER SIXTEEN

From the occupied and allied countries they came in the thousands; men, women and children. Transport that should have been used for the *Wehrmacht* was assigned to the Deathshead *Einsatzgrüppen*. Instead of men and munitions, human cargo. Langer and Teacher moved through the yards. Nausea filled them, their mouths tasting the bitter taste of vomit, barely held back. Truncheons were in widespread use as were pistols. The Germans were retreating, but they were making sure that they took with them all the human misery that they could. *The final solution must be carried out.* Jews, in their faces a strange mixture of fear and resignation, knowing where they were going, but not wanting to believe the unimaginable. By the hundreds they were pushed and packed into cattle cars until there was no room to stand. Mothers held their babies over their heads so they could breathe, but before the trains could unload, over half the people in each car would die of suffocation, or simply be crushed to death when they fell. SS guards, aided by enthusiastic Ukrainian police, went about their task in a businesslike manner, their faces devoid of any semblance of compassion or mercy; these were beasts who relished their work.

Sweat ran freely down Teacher's face, his eyes wide in their sunken sockets, skin waxy, pale, his hands trembling. The submeisser swung from its shoulder strap, bumping his leg with each step. "Carl," he half whispered hoarsely, his throat dry, "is this what we've become?"

A child cried, then silence. They passed a group of laughing SS and their Ukrainian counterparts standing in a huddle.

Teacher paused. "Carl, go on, I have something to do and I know you can't help me. Go on, you'll find your destiny later alone, as you always have."

Langer stopped, face grim; the beginning look of killing gathered at the corners of his eyes. Teacher gave a gentle shove with his hand.

"No, Carl, this is the way I want it. You told me once that life is a great circle with no beginning or end. Well, my circle has turned long enough. It's time for me to make a new beginning. Please go on, get away from me, now is not the time for you, it's mine and if you don't go I can't do it."

Langer sighed deeply, put his arms around the shoulders of the thin, sad-faced man and hugged him farewell. Silent, he walked away, not looking back. He passed between a couple of cars and their cargos of pain out of sight.

* * *

Teacher unslung his submachine gun, pulled the cocking lever back slowly. His back straightened, he held the gun to his hip, barrel straight ahead. He moved to where the SS and their toadies were enjoying themselves. Stopping at about fifteen meters, he called out, voice crackling, *"Kamaraden."*

The heads turned, curious at first at the intrusion. Then they saw the weapon pointed at them. "Heil Hitler, *Kamaraden."* The Schmeisser spoke its rapid, flat, cracking chatter; the bullets smashed into the packed group, dropping them to the earth to twitch and die, wondering at their pain. They weren't supposed to be hurt, they were the ones who gave pain, not received it. Teacher emptied the magazine on full auto, spraying the twitching bodies until they were still.

He dropped the weapon to the dirt, reached into his coat pocket, took out a grenade, knelt down and pulled the pin, holding the lever tight, tears running down his face into his beard. He raised his eyes to the gray skies. "God," he cried, "forgive me, God, that I didn't do this sooner."

Two SS *Sturmmen* seeing him on his knees from the back, with his gun lying beside him, rushed to throw themselves on this traitor; they reached him seconds after he released the hammer; they grabbed him in time to participate in the dull thud of the grenade's explosion, and died with him. Teacher crumpled over on his back, stomach almost completely ripped out, eyes wide; but for the first

time in years his face was calm; he found his way to
end the pain.

When the firing started Langer hesitated, started
to turn back, then stopped again. No, this was
Teacher's to do alone the way he wanted it. He had
no right to interfere. The crump of the Grenade
going off told him it was over. He walked on out of
the yards across to the road, where columns of men
fresh from Germany were being herded up to the
lines to fill gaps that couldn't be replaced with ten
times their numbers. Bright young faces, full of
confidence in the final victory. They knew the
Führer would triumph and they would show those
who went before them how to fight; all it took was
the proper spirit and faith.

Carl moved on, his feet automatically taking him
in the direction of the fighting, his body moving
under its own accord, following the built-in patterns of years of conflict; at times battle did ease
pain and the Russians he knew were no better than
the Nazis, so what difference did it make who he
killed?

Another winter was here; snow was in the air. His
greatcoat fluttered around his legs, the pack on his
back tugged familiarly at his shoulders, giving a hot
spasm of tension in the muscles between the shoulder blades. He walked with his eyes on the road,
joining in with the masses moving up. The steady,
kilometer-eating step of the professional took over
his subconscious and moved him. All that day, faces
picked at the corners of his mind. A sense of emp-

tiness all too familiar walked with him. The road
turned to slush with a cold drizzle falling which softened the ground, and the treads of armor and
trucks turned it into boot-sucking slush. Still, he
moved on to the distant sound of thunder. With the
dark, the first snow came, soft, fat white flakes that
floated gently, melting at first, then increasingly
one added its whiteness to another until the ground
was covered. The temperature dropped, the mud
began to firm, the snow fell steadily, one inch, then
another. Before midnight he stopped and took
shelter in a burned-down tavern. The beams were
still holding, made of oak hundreds of years old.
Time had turned them almost into iron; charred
and discolored they still held up part of the roof.
Langer settled into a corner. There, sheltered from
the snow, he built a small fire in a forgotten metal
wash pan and hunched over it, the red glow bouncing off his face, the warmth pressing against whatever skin was exposed. He leaned over to soak it in.
Taking his blanket out of his pack he wrapped it
around him; sitting Indian fashion, he nodded and
slept fitfully, head bobbing and jerking up for an
instant, eyes opening, then just as fast, shutting
again. Several times the waning fire woke him to
feed it and restless sleep claimed him again, only to
plague him with dreams and doubts.

The soldier's mental clock pulled his head up,
eyes open, fully awake. Just before dawn the night's
snowfall had reached five inches and the road was
gone, vanished under its covering; only the trees
and brush lining the way showed where it lay under
the blanket of white. Scrounging through the rub-

ble he found another battered tin pot. Filling it with fresh snow, he sat it by his fire to melt and warm him at the same time. Eating a ration, taking small bites of black bread, he held each bit in his mouth until it turned sweet and dissolved and he washed it down with a swallow of lukewarm ersatz coffee that tasted more like burned nut shells than anything else.

The Knight's Cross sparkled in the light of the fire as he took off his coat and tunic to wash in the melted snow water. Careful not to use too much of his remaining piece of soap, he gave himself what was known in less than polite circles as a whore's bath. Using a straight razor, he scrapped at the stubble on his face, cursing at the tugs and nicks. Drying himself with one of his dirty undershirts, he redressed. A momentary flick of consternation ran across his face when he put the Knight's Cross back on. But what the hell did it matter.

Thousands of passing trucks and men pulled him out on to the road. The rusting hulks of burned vehicles and tanks, both German and Russian, were common; relics from last year's battles, rusting skeletons that gave a sense of foreboding to those who saw them for the first time. For Carl Langer, they weren't even there.

Shortly after noon he stopped to rest in the shelter of a burned MK IV. Leaning up against the rusting bogie wheels, he eased off his pack and lit up, holding his hand cupped over the match to keep the wind from blowing it out. He looked at the sky. It would be dark soon, now probably around five o'clock. He had a few more hours before packing it in; there was no rush, if he didn't move fast enough it was a sure thing the war could come to him. A passing *Kübelwagen* with three men and a woman in it stopped beside him. The woman caught his eye. The fact that she had been worked over was obvious from the swelling around her left eye and bruised mouth. Her escorts were members of a special counter-guerrilla detachment of the SS. Tough-looking men, still wearing the distinctive SS leopard camouflage field jackets and helmet covers. The leader of the group, a *Hauptsturmführer* with a broken nose and crystal blue eyes, beckoned him over with a wave of the hand.

The SS captain beckoned Langer to him with a snap of the fingers. "Papers!"

Carl presented his paybook and movement orders to the "Golden Knight" of the new order, standing at attention. He glanced through the documents and quickly took in the decorations Langer had around his neck.

"Good enough, climb on, I have a job for you, it won't take long."

Langer knew better than to try and argue. Tossing his pack on the *Kübelwagen*, he climbed into the rear of the vehicle with the woman and her guards; it was crowded but the best they could do.

The jeep ran down the road for a few kilometers and turned on to a side road; headed into the trees for a couple of hundred meters and stopped. The *Hauptsturmführer* led the way up a narrow tree-lined trail to a log cabin. Standing back he let one of his men enter the door first; after all, one could never tell where one might find a booby trap, and enlisted men were expendable and easier to replace than officers. Once inside, one of the *Sturmen* built a fire in the rock fireplace, and stood by waiting for orders from his leader.

The captain pointed a gloved finger at Carl. "Sergeant, you will remain here with the prisoner until we return. We have to pick up a few more of the lady's compatriots being held for us further on. If she tries to escape, stop her any way you wish, but don't trust the treacherous bitch, she killed two of my men earlier today and we only caught her when a rifle grenade knocked her out and those that were with her left her behind. And besides," he said in a comradely fashion, "she's a Jew."

With a snap of his fingers, his men headed for the door. He seemed to have finger snapping down to a science; it wasn't easy to do with gloves on. Before leaving, he turned once more to Langer and in an off-handed way added, "Oh, by the way, if you like, you may use her for your amusement. After we return and have time to question her, we're going to hang her anyway, so enjoy yourself, comrade."

The sound of boots crunching their way off in the new snow soon diminished and they were left alone. Carl motioned for her to sit down in one of the two wooden straight-backed chairs at a plank table, careful to keep his weapons out of her reach. He had no idea about how dangerous a woman like this might be. He laid his pack down and sat in the other chair, taking a ration of black bread and a can of sardines out of his pack. He opened the tin and cut a slice of bread off and shoved them in front of her. "Eat! I'm not going to hurt you."

She warily reached for the food, her hunger overcoming her pride. She greedily stuffed the bread into her mouth, almost choking in her rush to swallow the food. Langer said nothing, just opened his canteen and handed it across the table to her. Choking, she swallowed a gulp of water, helping to force the coarse bread down her throat.

Softly, he spoke, "Take it easy, eat slow." He leaned back away from the table, aware of her feelings of hate for all who wore a uniform. Knowing the fear and hatred that was boiling inside her, he gave her time to relax and take some of the edge off as she finished eating and took the last swig of water. She screwed the red cap back on to the canteen and sat back. The swelling around her eye took nothing away from the defiance and hate showing there.

In good German, her voice clear and strong, if a little shaky around the edges, she asked, "What now, hero? Should I take my clothes off so you can be paid for the food?"

Langer shook his head. "No, I'm not going to do anything to you." He lit up a smoke and noticed the gleam in her eye.

"Want one?" He passed the pack and some matches over to her. Lighting up she let the smoke drift up into her nostrils and inhaled deeply, then exhaled the smoke slowly.

"Are you a Jew?"

Her head jerked up straight, her back erect as that of a British sergeant major. "Yes! I'm a Jew."

He nodded his head. "I thought so; even though the headhunters said you were, you can't always believe those sons of bitches."

She looked at him carefully; was this some kind of trick? For him to speak out against his own kind like this.

"No, I'm not one of them in spite of the uniform. I'm a soldier, not a butcher; there's no love lost between me and the SS supermen, especially those of the Allegemeine, although I have to admit the Waffen SS troops are about as tough as any I have ever seen. But their field troops are not garbage like the SD and SA." He could see the doubt in her eyes; there was one way that he might get through to her. "*Mah sheem-Hah?*" He asked her name in Hebrew. Startled she looked back and answered, "*Shem meesh-pakht-teh* Deborah Sapir. *Hah-Eev-reet-yoht Ah-Tenn?*"

"No, I'm not a Hebrew, though I did spend some time in Judea a long time ago."

The ice was broken; curiosity overcame some of her caution. She looked at the square-built figure as he took his coat off; the room was warming. True, he looked the part of a German, the close-cropped hair and scarred face, and there was something brutal about him, but it wasn't that insane cruelty of the SS or NKVD. His was that of a hunting animal who kills only for survival, not pleasure. There was something else too. She looked deep into the gray-blue eyes; behind them lay a great sadness, a feeling of terrible isolation and weariness. She shook her head to clear these feelings, as if she had almost been hypnotized. Taking a bite from his own chunk of bread, he chewed slowly, thinking. He caught her looking at the medals he wore, the fear and suspicion coming back. He leaned back in his chair and spoke softly, but in a direct way, to her. "Don't let the uniform influence you. Most men are no different, no matter what color the uniform they wear. Most Germans are the same as men everywhere, with families that they love, but they, like the Russians, are victims of a few ambitious men, men gone insane seeking their immortality; and insanity is contagious, it can drive those about them mad with the same sickness of mind and spirit.

"Those who fight this war, the soldiers, are caught up in that madness. It's too big to resist, and now they're committed to see it through to the end; it's gone too far to back away. I believed in the war in the beginning for reasons of my own. I felt that Russia had to be stopped before she grew so strong that no power would ever be able to resist her. The Communists are no better than the Nazis, they both feed on fear and power, but as wrong as the war was to start with, it has to go on a while longer. I know Germany is losing; the Allies have landed back on the European continent. Italy is almost gone, and every day we have fewer men to face the hordes of Russians that come at us."

Deborah watched him closely; there was no doubt in her mind that he was telling the truth as he saw it. "But why then do you continue to fight, don't you want the war to end?"

He nodded. "Yes, it's about time for this one to come to a halt, but not yet." He lit up another cigaret. "You see, the job now, though it will cost thousands of lives, is to bleed the Soviets as dry as we can every day, and hold them back long enough to give the British and Americans time to advance further into Europe and give more civilians time to escape to the West, ahead of the Russians. If we stopped now, there would be no stopping them, they would overrun all of Europe. In his own mind, Stalin is the Genghis Khan of this century and he wants to achieve what every conqueror has always wanted, to be master of the world and all that's in it. Hitler is no different, perhaps only a little madder."

She still didn't understand fully; consternation showed in her facial expressions. "If that's true, why did you fight to start with?"

He sucked on his smoke and blew the residue out of his nostrils. "In the beginning, as I told you, I believed the great lie, too. I have fought the hordes before. I believed, as did most of the other Germans, that war was inevitable between the West and Asia.

"It was felt that the Soviets would someday advance with all the hordes of Asia at their command, to loot and destroy the Western nations. They had to be stopped by a united Europe if civilization was to survive, and not drop back into the dark ages. I couldn't believe that the Germans I knew were capable of the horrors that they later inflicted on the world, but by then, it was too late to stop. You just had to go on and hope for the best, and there was some indication that Hitler would not outlast the assassination attempt by members of the general staff, but somehow the madman survived. So now I wait, and do what I can. One man can never really do a great deal; everything is too big, you're lost among the rules and regulations, the habits of training and survival take over; you're just too small to fight insanity on a scale the size of this, so I go on. But recently a friend of mine died to prove something, and now I think it's time for me to try another way, to separate myself from the masses of this holocaust, although what I will do will have little, if any, real effect on the outcome."

Rising, he stretched his arms and put another log on the fire, turning his back to the flames. The heat felt good against the back of his legs. "And you! What about you, Deborah Sapir?"

Deborah thought carefully before answering; what difference did it make if he were lying, the SS were going to kill her anyway. "I was at Auschwitz for six months; the officers liked my looks so they let me live. I was being taken to entertain at a party for one of them when the car was ambushed by partisans. Since that time I have been with different organizations trying to do what we could to save the Jews remaining; there are very few left now."

Langer moved a little bit away from the fire; it was growing too warm on the back of his legs. "Tell me what it was like there, I have to know." He moved to the table and sat opposite her again.

Her eyes took on a vacant expression; the words came by themselves. She became an instrument for the sake of the pain and suffering that poured out; she had been a whore for the SS, not because she was afraid to die, but because they paid her off with her life and food, some of which she gave to the children in the camp.

Through her eyes, he was drawn into the hell that was Auschwitz. Watching children torn from their mothers' arms and herded together to pass under a horizontal rod; those tall enough to touch it would live, for a while longer at least. Those too small were sent to the gas chambers immediately. Through the tears, he saw the young ones trying to stretch their necks, standing on tiptoe; anything to make them a little taller. The children knew somehow that something terrible awaited those who failed to touch that horrible high marker. The cries and screams, the stench of the ovens burning the waste that had once been people, while in the background the prison band played overtures from Schubert and Paganini. The tears running down her face, dropping on the table, made pools of sorrow for all mankind.

He saw it all, the dark clouds that hung constantly over the camp. The ashes from the ovens that fell, even into what little food they had. But it was the faces of the children that tore at his mind. The children, always it is the children; the innocents stand out the most. They danced for the amusement of the SS officers and sang sweet songs of the fields and valleys. Then they were gassed. The Panzer Soldier cried. From within, his life source, came a groan that transcended anything he had ever felt. Great choking sobs tore at him as the children spoke to him from Deborah's tears; the Old One cried.

The creaking of the door hinges swung him

around; the SS *Hauptsturmführer* stepped inside shaking his shoulders loose from the snow. His two henchmen followed. The officer stepped forward to where Deborah sat, his face full of anticipation; he grabbed her by the hair.

"Well, Jew bitch, it's time to go. Your three friends didn't take long to tell us all they knew. They're down the road a little ways waiting for your arrival." He laughed, enjoying himself. "They won't go anywhere for a while, though, so we have time to entertain you a bit first. You know the fat one? Well, he's at least four inches taller now than before. I suppose the extra weight made his neck stretch further than the others."

Not looking, he asked the Panzerman, "Did you enjoy yourself, comrade?"

He barely had time to notice the tanker's movement before the steel body of the Schmeisser crushed into his face, spreading his grin into a bloody smile as the bone crunched under the blow and the jawbone splintered.

The two SS men froze for a second, then the taller of the two started to swing his weapon up to fire, only to feel cold-burning pain as Langer's bayonet sunk into his stomach. He gave one weak whimper for his mother and fell. The other raised his above his head wanting to surrender.

But Langer was beyond any act of mercy. The pleading was cut off as scarred strong hands went around his throat and raised him from the floor, shaking him like a dog.

Tears ran in rivers as Langer shook until the SS man was no more than a crooked-necked broken doll waiting to be picked up and thrown away.

The *Haupsturmführer* gurgled through his broken face as he tried to raise himself up from the floor on to his hands and knees. Turning, Langer gave him one solid kick under the chin, snapping the man's head back until the vertebrae crushed in on each other.

The force of the kick flipped him over on his back. The grinning Deathshead insignia on his collar tab leered happily at another victim. Langer stood there empty-handed, stoop-shouldered and drained.

The touch of a gentle hand on his shoulder brought him back to his senses. Deborah stood watching, her face torn with sorrow. "We have to go now," she spoke as she would have to a child. "We have to go before anyone else comes."

Nodding weakly, he picked up the weapons from the floor and took the officer's pistol and stuck it into his own belt. He gave her one of the MP-40s and slung another over his shoulder. He knew they would need them before long. He had another war to fight now.

Deborah led him by the hand out of the hut into the snow, leaving the SS men to be found later. Their feet crunched on the frozen surface layer and then sunk down to ankle deep. They moved into the darkness of the woods; their tracks would soon be covered by the gently falling large clean flakes. As they walked, Langer ripped the patches from his uniform and threw them along with his paybook and orders into the snow. Last to go was the Knight's Cross from around his neck. He let it fall from limp fingers and sink into the softness, the silver edges gleaming until it too was covered.

By the end of January the German forces had withdrawn to the western banks of the Oder River. Pursued not only by the Russians but also by a man and a woman who made their prey the *Einsatz-grüppen* of the SS. Like wolves they hunted the straggling units of the Totenkopf or SD.

From Langer, Deborah learned more than she would have dreamed of about the fine art of killing. How to place a mine or strangle a man larger than yourself with a fine piece of wire. Time and again they had eliminated parties of SS herding their helpless prisoners back to the loading pens for shipment to the concentration camps.

Langer grew wolflike in appearance, face lean and hard with no trace of pity for the butchers he relentlessly hunted and killed.

In this battle, mercy was a commodity they had not earned. Though many asked for it, no one received it. The bayonet and garrote snuffed out the life of the hunted silently, or the single crack of a well-placed shot, taking out the leader of a party escorting prisoners. Langer and Deborah lived off the land, taking whatever they could scavenge or steel. This was their crusade, their "Jihad," Holy War, and with the dedication of a religious zealot they spared none, not even themselves. They pushed on.

The SS in charge of the final-solution program began to get nervous about venturing too far from the safety of their headquarters. Several high-ranking officers had gone on inspection trips to make sure the Führer's orders were being obeyed, never to return, or if they were found, to be silent testimony that someone was carefully and selectively eliminating them as they did the Jews. The feeling was definitely unpleasant.

The memory of how many times they had struck vanished from their minds. There was no limit, no thought of doing just so much and no more. They continued to live in burned-out buildings or holes in the ground, trying to keep up with the retreating Germans and ahead of the Russians, who would suffer the same fate as the SS if they happened to get too close. As for Deborah and Langer, there was little difference in them, but their chosen prey were those in the black uniforms and swastika armbands. At night they would hold each other for warmth, and what comfort they had came from each other. They loved in a special kind of way that made them twins or extensions of each other. There was tenderness for Deborah in the arms of the scar-faced man, a gentleness she would not have believed when she first saw him. She knew that he had suffered great pain in his life that made him different in a thousand small ways from the men she had known. He was timeless in his patience with her, taking hours to explain a small detail that could mean her survival. About his own survival, he really didn't seem to be very interested, as long as he could accomplish what he set out to do. Each mission, each ambush, was a thing unto itself, which might end everything for them. Every act itself was a complete statement.

The greatest difficulty they had was choosing a

good target area in order to kill the SS before they could kill the prisoners with them. He taught Deborah the use of selective terror tactics and to use lies, false hope and illusion. A single truck with eight Jews and four guards; one beside the driver and two in the back with their cargo. A shot to blow a tire, another to kill the driver; a burst of machine-gun fire from Deborah on the opposite side to convince them that they were surrounded, and promise the SS their lives, if they freed the prisoners. If they did, once the prisoners were well away, they'd kill the guards. Honor meant nothing to the SS, and a man or woman would be a fool to trust their word. Also, to let them live would condemn still more innocents to the slaughter. This was total war as Hitler wanted it. Death, the final solution.

Langer rested under the shelter of a giant pine; the branches heavy with snow made a natural tent to shelter them. He slept with his head on Deborah's lap. It was the hour before dawn, and she too slept the deep sleep of exhaustion.

Alsatians put their noses to the light breeze and tugged their masters forward silently. The *Hundmeisters* knew they were near.

Their dogs had their vocal chords cauterized to make certain there would be no giveaway barking to let their quarry know of their presence. The squad of counter-guerrilla experts was spread out in skirmishing formation, weapons ready; only the crunching of booted feet in the snow broke the silence. A distant cough brought Langer to full awakening; his eyes snapped open, alert, ready. He rolled off Deborah's lap, his movement waking her.

"Shhhh!" He looked out between the branches of their shelter. First one then another, then five and another five spread out, moving in good order, very professional. He looked to the left, then the right; on both sides the flankers had already passed their tree and were slightly behind them. The hunters were damned good.

Langer nodded his head in mental agreement with what he knew would come some day. He pulled Deborah to him, wiped a smudge from her face and kissed her with the gentleness of a brother and lover. Whispering, he told her what to do; with a finger, he touched her lips and silenced her protests. "This I must do, you can't help me now." He reached into his pack and took out a vial of powder and gave it to her. "Climb into the tree; when they go after me, come down and sprinkle this around the base where we were sleeping. I've been saving this for some time; it's cocaine mixed with dried blood. When the dogs smell it the cocaine will make them high and knock out their sense of smell for hours. Use that time to get away. Find a place and hole up; we've done all we can. As for me, don't worry. Save yourself, the war will be over soon, it's only a matter of a few months at most. Save yourself, Deborah Sapir, and remember me as one who loved you well."

He burst out of the trees, his Schmeisser cutting down three men on the right flanking squad. He hit the snow and rolled over, taking out the other two; one side was open. He turned and faced the oncoming *Hundmeisters*. Roaring he charged, wild-eyed, gun firing. He emptied one magazine and reloaded.

Two *Hundmeisters* were dead, their animals whimpering beside the bodies, their leashes around their dead masters' hands, keeping them from attacking, but Langer still kept on racing from tree to tree. A burst of fire from the SS men ripped up the bark and sent splinters stinging into the side of his face. He twisted and dodged, turning and leaping; anything to draw them away from Deborah. He made a hundred meters, then another, stopping to reload and fire. They closed in on him.

A hurtling object caught the corner of his eye and he knew it was too late to get away. The thrower had a damned good arm; it would burst in the air. The concussion grenade exploded four feet from him in the air, peppering his face and driving the darkness into him, blocking out his consciousness. His last thought before the explosion was, "Did I get them far enough away?" He had.

As soon as they took off after him, Deborah had climbed down from her perch and followed his instructions and sprinkled the ground with the cocaine and blood. The dogs that came after they handcuffed Langer were useless for two days. Deborah looked back once, the cold freezing her tears as she choked them back. He had done what he had to do. Now she must go on and do what he wanted her to do. She would live to see that every Nazi butcher was found and punished. "Shalom, Carl, Shalom."

The counter-guerrilla experts loaded their unconscious prize into the back of a Krupp three-ton six-by-four with a canvas covering to keep out the weather. Inside they made use of the chains and

manacles brought along for this purpose. They had
been assigned to bring in the man named Carl
Langer and to bring him in alive. The orders came
directly from Gestapo headquarters in Berlin. As to
his companion, they could care less; they had what
they had come after and according to their orders
had chained him securely, hands and feet.

At Elbing they turned him over to a special escort
party from the Sicherheitsdienst, tough-looking
men, well fed and confident. The guerrilla fighters
looked on them with some distaste. They took pride
in the fact that next to the famed unit, under the
command of Col. Otto Skorzeny, they were the best
that the SS had to offer. The badge on their breast
pocket was a sword with a serpent twisted around
the blade. The SS men from Berlin had no decorations other than their written authority, which was
enough to have even generals shot on the spot.
They were glad to see them go.

Langer had awakened about halfway back during
the bumpy three-hour ride through the forests and
fields. Several times they had pulled over under the
shelter of the trees to avoid the searching eyes of
Russian fighters, then moved on. His whole body
ached from head to toe, the concussion grenade had
nearly burst his eardrums, and both eyes were
swollen almost shut and red with ruptured veins.
His escort said nothing to him, they had their orders, silence; no one was to talk to or question the
prisoner on threat of pain of death. What he had
done to bring down on him the personal wrath of
the highest levels of the Gestapo was beyond their
understanding. As far as they knew, he was just an-

other turncoat traitor who had done a bit of sniping.

The SD men sat silently, one on each side of their prisoner, in the rear of the Daimler Benz 230. The driver and man riding shotgun kept their eyes on the road, but seemed to have selective blindness; an occasional body dangled from a tree or telegraph pole with a sign around its neck, reading "Collaborator" or "Coward." All this was unnoticed. They passed through several checkpoints manned by their kindred.

Who even looked at their brothers with hungry eyes, as if regretful that they had proper papers for heading to the rear. Only the sight of their manacled and chained guest gave them any sense of satisfaction. At least there was another traitorous bastard going to his just rewards. They were waved on while the headhunters checked the papers of a Luftwaffe colonel and gleefully began to slap him around, ignoring his protests of rank and privilege. The colonel was still protesting when they shot him in the neck and strung him up a freshly printed sign reading, "Traitor to the Reich." The SD loved sticking it to the officers, especially those who looked like they had come from the Junker's class. You were in serious trouble if you wore a monocle even if you had proper papers.

The civilian population of East Prussia was in flight, heading back to the borders of Germany. They knew they would be safe there, the Führer had promised it.

The silence was broken only by the sounds of the SD men stuffing their faces with sausage and bread, gurgling it down with white wine. The prisoner was given nothing and he was nothing but dead meat anyway. If nothing else, he did give them a reason to put some distance between them and the advancing Russian hordes.

Langer's face was drawn and thin from days of little rest, which had worn him down to a ragged, thin-faced wretch who didn't look to be particularly dangerous, especially in chains. That is, until you looked close at the eyes and the steel-set jaw; then you knew the man was a chained animal, capable of tearing your arms off with his bare hands. Yes, the animal definitely needed to be properly restrained.

Spring was close, and green shoots stuck their heads up through patches of melting snow. Life in its endless cycle of birth and death was not to be denied; it went on. Langer rode for the most part with his eyes closed, getting what rest he could. He knew when they reached Germany there would be little of that for him. One town after another fell behind them and the waves of panic-stricken civilians thinned to a trickle. They felt safe here, but the soldiers knew different; the war was finished and the Russians were going to bleed Germany until there was nothing left. The Russian soldiers had been promised as their reward the women of Germany and everything they could carry off. It was to be the greatest rape in history.

The bumping of the car jogged his memory. They were all gone now, Teacher, Manny, Yuri and Stefan, all gone except for Gus, that rambling bear of a man. A tick at the corner of Langer's face tried to turn into a smile but failed. The last time he had seen Gus alive was outside of Osterode when the headhunters were taking him back; he was strolling down the road heading back to Germany with a pig following him on a leash, the pig blissfully ignorant of its destiny. Yes, Gus was heading back home singing off key as loud as he could, the familiar strains of "Ich hat eine Kamaraden," keeping time with a bayonet. How he had gotten past the headhunters, Langer could only guess. But if anyone could get back it would be Gus. Langer wished him well; at least there would be one left.

They reached the border of Germany the next morning. The immaculate border guards checked their papers and waved them through. At Landsberg they handed their cargo over to an *Obersturmnführer* with the insignia of the Totenkopf Deathshead Unit on his collar and made their exit. Even they did not want to hang around any longer than necessary. This place had the antiseptic odor of a clinic, a place dealing with death and pain.

The *Obersturmnführer* adjusted steel-rimmed glasses and peered at the documents stating the prisoner's case. Taking his time and pursing his lips and clicking his tongue over several times, while Langer stood at rigid attention (old habits die hard), *Obersturmnführer* Meyer removed his glasses and rose from his desk. Shaking his head from side to side, he walked around the object of his attention, keeping a slight distance, not from fear but because the prisoner hadn't bathed in some time and still wore the mud of the eastern front on him. "You are really in a lot of trouble." The words were spoken gently and quietly. "You really are,

173

you know. I don't know why they had you brought
back here anyway, you should have just been shot
where they found you, but orders are orders." He
chuckled. "Ours not to reason why, ours but to do
or die, *nicht war?* and my orders read that you are
to be sent on from here." He rapped on the door
and two SS men entered. Pointing to Langer, he
said, "Take him, have him cleaned up and give him
a fresh uniform with no insignia. Army! not SS! and
keep him chained at all times. You may remove the
manacles only when he is dressing; he's dangerous
according to his files. However, he is not to be
harmed in any way except by a higher authority,
though God knows why. Remove him!"

Langer had to endure the humiliation of a complete body search, which meant every hole and
orifice of his body was checked by rubber-gloved
guards who poked and prodded, feeling for anything such as a tube of money concealed in the rec-
tum or a poison capsule hidden in a tooth, but there
was nothing, and half reluctantly they gave up their
efforts and permitted the prisoner to dress after
being deloused and scrubbed. He was fed white
bread from the SS kitchen and given chicken in a
cream sauce with vegetables. He ate with a spoon,
as he was not permitted to use any sharp instru-
ments. It was the first solid food he had eaten in
four days and he had had nothing as exotic as white
bread or stewed chicken for months. He almost
threw it back up.

He was transported by truck to a nearby field and
loaded along with his escort into a HE-111 con-
verted for troops or passengers from its regular use

as a bomber. Staying out of the corridors that the allies used for bombing runs on Germany, they winged high over the Fatherland, peaceful now from this distance; but below a nation was dying. After a flight of several hours, they touched down, the wheels screeching as the brakes gripped and dug in to stop the Heinkel. A Mercedes was waiting at the door when they stopped. Two more SS men with machine pistols in readiness stood by on motorcycles to escort the car and its passengers into the mountains. Langer noted carefully concealed bunkers that housed antitank guns and heavy machine guns all along the route leading to their destination. All the crews wore the camouflage patterns peculiar to the SS.

Stahlberg Castle rose out of the morning mist, a remnant left over from the feudal days of Germany. It looked more like a picture postcard than a real building. Strong, massively built from the native mountain stones, it had lasted centuries with little change, probably much less change than humanity had achieved since the bloody days of its construction. The Stahlberg. Even the name sounded ominous.

The terrain immediately adjacent to the castle was well guarded by the elite fanatics of the SS regiment Adolf Hitler. Young faces that had known defeat watched him through serious eyes. Their commanders were battle-tested veterans of Russia and Europe that had somehow managed to retain their fanaticism for the New Order even in the face of disaster. They had no god but Adolf Hitler and as with religious fanatics, to die in the service of your god was the greatest accomplishment one could hope for. They had the look of martyrs about them, men seeking their own perverse form of paradise and ready to kill or be killed for it.

Once inside the Stahlberg, the atmosphere changed to one of a time long past. Arms and armor lined the halls. Flags and pennants of battles long forgotten added bits of faded color to the gray stone. Interspersed were badly done paintings of the castle's former masters, with stern, righteous faces that glowered down on all who passed beneath as if sitting in judgment.

The floors were polished by a couple of Polish slaves who kept their eyes averted from those of their overlords. Slaves were not permitted to look directly at a member of the master race without permission. They too waited with a resignation to their own coming finality. They knew that they would never live to return home even if the Germans lost the war. They were dead men, they merely hadn't been buried yet, but knew that time was drawing close.

The escorting officer rapped once sharply on a single door, waited a moment and ushered his charge inside to stand in front of a plain, businesslike desk devoid of ornamentation except for a single telephone. The walls were bare save for the black and silver flag of the SS standing in the right corner.

More impressive was the man behind the desk, *Brigadeführer* Erich Zeitsler wearing the uniform of the Waffen SS, the only uniform in the castle that wasn't black. Around the neck he wore the Knight's

Cross with oak leaves and swords. The only other decoration to break the plainness of the uniform was a gold party badge. The man's face had none of the look of the fanatic common to the rest of the staff he had seen. The face was strong, square jawed under close-cropped, graying, ash-blond hair. Pale-blue eyes looked him over with obvious curiosity. Intelligent, cold eyes. With a flick of his hand he dismissed the escort, leaving them alone.

The SS general indicated for his guest to sit in the single wooden-back chair in front of his desk. Langer's manacles clanked as he obeyed the unspoken order.

Langer cast a quick look around the stone-walled room, noting a single window set about five feet from the floor. Zeitsler smiled and spoke for the first time, his voice steady, the words measured and precise. He shook his finger schoolmasterishly. "I really wouldn't consider it if I were you. It's a sixty-foot drop to the ground, where you would land in a stone courtyard in which a machine gun and its crew are positioned. And if you somehow managed to free yourself from your chains and take me prisoner it would still serve no purpose. My guards have their orders and they wouldn't hesitate a heartbeat to shoot me down to stop you, Herr Longinus."

Langer froze at the name. "You have me mistaken, Herr *Brigadeführer*, my name is Langer, Carl Langer."

Zeitsler smiled and shook his head, opening a desk drawer. He removed the contents. Several photographs were visible from where Langer sat and some older documents looking like parchment, old, very old. His heart skipped a beat. He sat tense, fully alert, awaiting the next move with a definite feeling of foreboding pervading the atmosphere of the sterile office.

"You may relieve yourself of playing at charades. We know exactly who you are." He tapped the folder. "It's all in here, including the report of your stay at the sanctuary of Elder Dacort. Indeed, we know all about you. How long has it been since you were called by your true name, Casca Rufio Longinus? No matter." He waved a hand dismissing the unimportant thought. "We have been looking for you for some time now. We lost sight of you in the twenties when the world went to pieces following the depression. But when we received your name from the Geheime Staats Polizei they also sent along your paybook, which they found after you killed three of our men. With that a complete investigation was launched as a matter of routine. There is no Carl Langer. You took the name from a tombstone in Bayreuth and acquired your other papers after that. Indeed, we have been awaiting your arrival for some time. You would be flattered to know how many man-hours and how much money have been spent on seeing that you could join us. Indeed, you have arrived at a most opportune time." He checked his watch. "In a few minutes all your questions will be answered. In the meantime you will remain in this room until someone comes for you. You are our guest and food will be brought. But please, no tricks. We know all about—how should we say it?—your condition." He laughed softly. "And as you know, there are worse things than dying." He left closing the door behind him, but Langer knew he was being watched. The general's words echoed in his mind, worse things than dying . . . Sweat broke out on his forehead.

Did the SS general know? And if so, to what purpose was he brought here? What could the SS want with him? Questions, too many of them.

No longer thinking of himself as Carl Langer, Casca Longinus rose from his seat and looked over the papers on the desk. He knew the general had left them out in the open for that purpose. The story, the truth, was there. Not everything, but enough. They did know.

There was nothing to be used in the room as a weapon. Even the flagpole would be of little use against the machine guns and hundreds of men here who would just overpower him. And as the general said, there were worse things than dying. He sat back down to wait.

Langer felt familiar with the stone walls of the medieval castle. He passed stone-faced guards standing rigidly at their posts with faces pale in the glow of the bare light bulbs, spaced every ten or so feet throughout the halls of the castle. Unsmiling, serious faces that stood in pale deathlike contrast to the black of their dress SS uniforms, each armed with a Schmeisser machine pistol slung from the shoulders by the straps ready for instant use, as was evidenced by the fact that the cocking levers were drawn full back ready to instant firing. They knew they were chosen, the elite. Ready to die for the Führer, God and the Reich.

His escort had the same vacuous expressions, the

dead eyes, that would only come alive when they were witnessing the pain of another. They halted at the end of one corridor before massive, ancient wooden doors carved with the mystic runic symbols of the ancient Nordics, a stylized oak tree wrapped about with the twining tendrils of the great serpent. Standing in front of the Laers he felt a sense of foreboding that there was something evil behind the doors.

The guards escorting stopped, the one on the right raised a massive brass knocker in the shape of a Viking's head and let it drop once. The sharpness of the heavy brass head striking sounded once, heavily. The two guards then placed themselves one on each side of the door facing back down the hallways they had come from. Not a word had been spoken in the time since they had taken him from his rooms, and it appeared there would be none now.

With no sound the well-oiled hinges worked smoothly, holding the massive weight of the single door that swung to the inside. From the darkened interior came but one short command: Enter.

The door swung silently shut behind him, leaving him and the voice in a small anteroom lit only by the flickering glow of two oil braziers giving off a lightly pungent, scented aroma. The voice belonged to a man dressed in monk's habit resembling those the Franciscan monks wore, dark rough cloth. A hood covered the face so the features were indistinguishable in the gloom. A rope for a belt tied the waist loosely. The figure motioned for Langer to follow, leading him to a dark curtain of wine silk embossed with the symbols of the fish and cross.

The curtains parted. . . .

Langer's heart stopped for a moment with his throat constricting. . . . A line of oil braziers identical to those in the anteroom lined the aisle and the walls of the long narrow room, illuminating the fifty or so kneeling figures all dressed identically to the monk next to him, their backs turned, facing the end of the room.

All attention from the kneeling monks was focused at the end of the hall, where superimposed over a life-size wooden cross was . . . THE SPEAR . . . Mine, it's back again, am I forever to be haunted by not only the Jew but that damned thing, too?

One kneeling figure at the front detached itself from the line of worshipers, rose and walked down the aisle to face him. The face was hidden in the shadows, but there was a familiarity to the walk, the body english of the approaching monk.

A hand raised itself and moved the hood back to show the face. Round plain features with steel-rimmed glasses. Heinrich Himmler, *Reichführer* SS, spoke to his guest. "Welcome, Longinus, welcome to the Brother of the Lamb. It has been a long time since you were our guest. But as you see, we survived as you do, and whither thou goest so go we."

Taking Casca by the arm, he led him from the chamber through a side door and down a narrow hall to his personal chambers. Once inside he removed the cassock; underneath was the more familiar black uniform of the SS. . . . Motioning for Casca to sit, Himmler sat himself opposite him behind a plain wooden desk. The room was bereft of any ornamentation other than a single picture of Adolf Hitler sitting on Himmler's desk in a plain silver frame. Speaking softly, the head of the SS adjusted his glasses with a fingertip. "Well, now, Casca Rufio Longinus, I regret that we here at the Haven must be deprived of your company without first having a proper opportunity to show some old-fashioned hospitality."

Casca spoke for the first time. "What do you mean, in the weeks remaining?"

"The war is lost, and we have many things yet to do. Those brothers you saw in the chapel are the last of our order in Germany to be sent to other countries. This experiment is at an end and it has been for our purposes reasonably successful."

Noting the consternation on his guest's face, he continued. "Perhaps I should enlighten you a little on the matter. It won't make any difference if you know. It was the Brotherhood who brought Hitler to power, to serve our purposes, which were and are the destruction of the Jews, who next to you we detest above all things on this earth." A pious tone came into his voice. "You killed our Lord Jesus, but it was the Jews who made it possible; you were merely a tool. For that crime the Jews must be erased. That was the purpose of the final-solution program and it worked quite well for the short time we were in operation. Somewhere between five and six million of them have been eliminated; that accounts for about twenty-five percent of the total world Jewish population." He touched his finger tips together under his chin. "Not a bad start, would you say?"

Casca said nothing, merely stared in shock. For a soldier to kill was one thing, but the way this mild-looking man spoke of the deaths of millions who never had a chance to even defend themselves or fight back, was a horror his mind couldn't grasp.

Pleased at the effect he was having the Reich Führer continued. "Adolf Hitler was merely a member of the second circle of the Brotherhood and until forty-three we had him well under control.

"But then he began to think he was the real force and genius behind all that had taken place, and as you know, once he began to exercise his own judgment on military and political matters, the scene rapidly deteriorated. I must confess we were a little careless in letting him get so much personal control of things, but that's history or soon will be. And even now we must occasionally give in to his whims, at least, as I said, for the next few weeks. By then the war will be over and Hitler will be dead. So it is necessary to send you to Berlin. He wishes to see you.

"But have no fear, we will meet again. It may even be possible that I may be able to salvage something out of the defeat and take control of Germany again. I shall remain in the country to the end to see if that's possible. If it is not, then I too shall die. But the Brotherhood will not. We are in every country in the world preparing for the next round. Like you we have time on our side. What matters a few centuries so long as the desire is achieved?"

Casca cleared his throat, face grim. "And what is that?"

Himmler rose from behind his desk and touched one of a series of buttons on the corner. . . .

"Why, to establish a state church of the world which we will control. That's why it is necessary to break down all existing structures. Britain is finished as a world power. Her foreign empire will not long survive the death of Germany. The Catholic Church is in a state of complete ineffectiveness and that will continue until it will be something people will pay no more than lip service to. And the Jews . . ." For the first time venom accented his words. "We are not finished with them either. Anywhere you find anti-Semitism you find us close by, whether it is the Ku Klux Klan in America or the Spanish Inquisition, we will destroy them. Even now plans are being made for the use of other groups and races to aid us in the great work, and they like you will be only tools, never knowing they are merely puppets and dancing to the tugging of their strings by the Brotherhood."

His dialogue was interrupted by a short rap on the door. Himmler gave permission to enter, and the door opened. Zeitsler stood in the entrance with two guards behind him. "It's time to go, Elder, your plane's waiting."

Himmler sighed, and remarked, "No rest for the weary. You will remain here until I send for you. General Zeitsler, he will be your direct responsibility. *Auf Wiedersehen*, Herr Longinus."

The two guards stepped forward, tough, cold-looking men. One on each side, they left the

Reichführer's office. Turning he took one quick look at the man who had thrown the world into turmoil. He had returned to his desk sitting there. Mild mannered, unobtrusive, someone you would never look twice at on the street. Wiping the lenses of his glasses gently with a clean white handkerchief, murmuring softly to himself.

The closing of the door shut him out.

The guards escorted him back through the maze of corridors and halls downstairs, deeper into the bowels of the mountain. Guards were everywhere. There was none of the normal slack discipline that usually occurs when one has been out of action at a safe job for too long. These men were not bored, they were deadly in their intensity and devotion to duty.

He was shown into a room without windows, large enough that he wouldn't bump into himself, but that was about all there was except for a comfortable-looking single bed, a night stand, and a small table with a marble top that he presumed was what he would eat on.

When Langer inquired as to the length of his captivity, Zeitsler would merely say, "Patience, my dear man, what's a few weeks to you?" "I believe I know what the Elder"—he referred to Himmler in this manner when they were alone—"I believe the Elder has some definite plans for you that will require your leaving soon. Personally, I'll be glad when you do. I'm really not cut out for the role of a jailer. Once you leave I can return to my troops and at least be able to participate in the final struggle. Ah, death, where is thy sting?"

Several times medical personnel visited him to take blood and tissue samples. What they found out, he didn't know. Perhaps they were trying to learn why he was what he was. He really didn't know or care, but Zeitsler more than once upon reading the analysis of his examinations had whistled softly between his teeth, a thing he did only when he was truly amazed or surprised. February gave way to March and the war raged on again after its brief respite. This was the final blow. Germany would be once and for all completely destroyed, to never rise from the ashes they would leave her in.

A thousand bomber raids by the Americans followed by the huge night raids of the Royal Air Force pounded the major cities from the air while victorious armies swept in prisoners by the tens of thousands, men without weapons or fuel to resist the overwhelming logistical and material superiority that engulfed them. There were isolated victories in small actions for the Germans, but these only delayed the inevitable by minutes.

The SS continued to fight fanatically, usually to the last man or bullet. They knew full well what awaited them if they were taken alive, especially by the Russians. When they fought the Americans or British to the last bullet they would often surrender. When they fought the Russians to the last bullet, they saved it for themselves.

Breslau, Torun, and Poznan were surrounded and held out for a few weeks. But by the end of February, the Russians had a firm front in depth on the Oder River less than forty miles from Berlin.

Bulgaria, Romania, Poland, and most of Czechoslovakia and Yugoslavia were firmly under their control as well as part of Austria.

In the west, the Americans of General Hodges's 1st Army crossed the Rhine after capturing the Remagen bridge intact. The Netherlands, Belgium, France and Luxembourg were clear of German forces.

Langer waited out the weeks impatient, yet helpless, to do anything about it. One thing, though, that he had always had on his side was time. On 18 April, Zeitsler came for him with the word that he would be leaving. A Feisler Stroch had flown in and would be taking him to the field at Templehof in Berlin. Himmler would be awaiting his arrival. There was a special event about to occur and he didn't think Herr Langer would want to miss it.

The passenger seat in the light reconnaissance aircraft had been fitted with a special hookup to keep its passenger chained while in the aircraft. The flight was bumpy if uneventful until they neared Berlin. They had flown low, dipping in and out of the valleys until they hit the plains, and then stayed low to the ground, often flying at no more than four or five hundred feet. The pilot was good and took every measure to avoid the possibility of encountering American or Russian fighters. Night was approaching as they flew onto the field at Templehof. The smoke of the burning city could be seen for a hundred kilometers, but the full impact didn't hit until they made their approach onto the runway, passing over the gutted shell of the city that once housed millions. The Stroch touched down and quickly taxied into a protected concrete hangar.

Four members of the A.H. Leibstandarte awaited his arrival. They hustled into a Mercedes staff car and raced through the streets. Twice, Russian fighter bombers flew overhead and halfheartedly fired off a few rounds at the car and went on to easier, less mobile targets. A hospital off Wilmersdorf received their attentions and four hundred men burned alive in their beds. It was a hospital that specialized in the treatment of para- and quadraplegics.

The Mercedes had to make repeated changes to avoid streets that were blocked by the rubble of destroyed buildings until they could finally reach Wilhelmstrasse leading to the Reich Chancellery. From there, they parked the car in the shelter of the Reich Chancellery basement.

What the Soviets would call the Battle of Berlin had begun officially for them two days before. Thousands of guns pounded the city endlessly, one every thirteen feet around the perimeter.

Ivan was content for now to let the long range of his guns do the greater part of the killing. They knew that thousands of them would die in the street fighting. Let the guns do as much as they could first, they were in no hurry.

Following a passage, his escort led him down to a lower basement where a number of facilities were established. One in particular was guarded by tough professionals from the front. Entering, he once more led into the presence of *Reichführer* Himmler. In full uniform he rose from behind his desk and advanced to meet his visitor. "Free him." The order surprised Langer, but naturally he made no protest. Himmler ushered him to an overstuffed chair that had once graced one of the anterooms of the chancellery. "Sit," he called and an orderly brought Langer a glass of Black Forest Kirschwasser. Silent, he waited and sipped the cherry-flavored drink.

"It is so good to see you again, Herr Longinus. And now perhaps I will have time to fill you in on what is going to be happening to you while you are our guest. First, I have removed your bonds, for as the Elder Dacort knew, we know that it would not serve our purpose to have you confined or in chains. One never knows when the messiah may come again, now does one? And we have certainly done our best to create the conditions described in Revelations. But if he is going to come I fear he must hurry or it will be all over."

This then was to be his home until the *Reichführer* determined to what use he could be put. The only one permitted to speak to him was Zeitsler. The general kept him posted on the progress of the war.

Germany was almost at the end of its tether. The winter offensive against the Americans in the Ardennes had failed. The weather and stubborn resistance had slowed the German forces down until they had literally run out of fuel.

The Russians had, by the end of January, pushed the Germans back to the west side of the Oder and stood on the doorstep of the Reich itself. The next step would be the invasion of Germany, once supply lines and logistical support had caught up with the advance. Right now there would be another pause until the Russians could resupply and prepare for the final act.

Zeitsler was always courteous and well mannered if a little cynical. Langer wondered at a man of his intelligence being part of the mad order of the Brotherhood.

The general merely smiled and answered with a trace of humor. "Haven't you ever heard, Langer, if I may still use your German name—it's easier for me than Longinus—haven't you heard that there is no way to reason with religion or politics? It is enough that I believe in the mission of the Brotherhood as did my family for over three hundred years. Not quite as long as you have been around, to be sure, but still a long history of devotion and service that I quite agree with. A man, after all, has to live or die for something, doesn't he?"

He caught himself and laughed again.

He saw Himmler again the following day in the same office. The steady thumping crunch of artillery rounds landing was a constant reminder that war had come to Berlin. Dust fell from the ceilings in a steady thin mist covering everything with a powdery film. Only thirty thousand garrison troops were available for the defense of the capital, but the Russians knew the street fighting would be fierce, so they stood back and pounded.

The city was a gutted shell of its former glory, but all this meant little to the gentle-mannered man behind the desk. He had more important things on his mind.

Smiling, he looked up from some papers. "Well, now it's time to have a little chat. The reason I have brought you here is you are to be my birthday present to the Führer tomorrow. I know that you would not wish to miss such an important occasion, and he has requested that you be present. You understand, one man of destiny to another, that sort of thing. And it is still to my benefit to oblige him in these small matters.

"From your files, I see that you have given the Russians almost as much trouble as you did our people. Why?"

Langer explained his reasons the same as he had told Deborah in the hut.

Himmler bobbed his head in agreement. "I thought it would be something like that. Your character is somewhat predictable, you know. Where in all these centuries did you develop a sense of morality?"

Langer thought over the question for a few moments. "I don't really know. I do know that nothing I will ever do makes any real difference. But still if I must go on at least I can have the satisfaction of not degenerating into a child-killing animal like you."

Himmler wiped his glasses. "Insults will serve no purpose, since I really have no concern about your attitudes toward us. But understanding you as I do, I have given orders that you are to be released from your house arrest and issued weapons." Langer sat stunned.

"Why?"

Himmler smiled a secret smirk. "It's simple. Give

me your word that you will not use the weapons against me personally and I will set you free to do what you have always done best, fight.

"Surely now, at this place and time the best thing you could do would be to kill Russians. Everyone you eliminate saves a helpless person some misery. There are no Jews in Berlin for you to rescue. Hitler will die by his own hand shortly, and I will be done before you're permitted to have any weapons. So it amuses me to give you your freedom. But don't worry, we will be watching and will most certainly keep track of your movements in the future. Now, if you will excuse me, I have some matters to take care of."

The following morning, Casca was issued a new uniform, complete with his rank badges and decorations for service to the Reich. Casca attended the party in the company of SS *Reichführer* Himmler. The reception was being held at the Chancellery Ehrenhof, the traditional spot for the occasion. Casca thought about the word Ehrenhof, place of honor. Bullshit.

He received a number of strange looks from the assorted guests, but Himmler made no introductions and did not allow him to converse with anyone. Inside for the first time were the orchestrators of the war and their own disaster. The ministers who gave Hitler legal authority over the fate of millions.

Hermann Göring sailed through the guests, an overweight ship bemedaled and dressed in one of his elaborate parade uniforms, smiling and wishing everyone well on this auspicious occasion. The official affair lasted about an hour and there was no liquor served. The Führer was a teetotaler and a nonsmoker.

Langer watched the master of Germany move around greeting first one then another of his ministers, his face, drawn and haggard, looking more like that of a tired old man who should have been in a rest home rather than the leader of the victorious German legions.

Himmler checked his watch. "Time for me to go." Casca looked at him questioningly. "One moment, please." Himmler signaled to a Lieutenant of *Führerbegleitkommando*, Hitler's personal bodyguard from the SS.

Clicking his heels, the junior officer stood at rigid attention.

Himmler made the introductions.

"*Stabsfeldwebel* Langer, may I present *Obersturmführer* Joachim Wolff, a member of my personal staff now assigned to the FBK during these trying times. He will a little later present you to the Führer and afterwards see to your being given weapons and whatever gear you may desire.

"I will now go and present my felicitations to the Führer and take my leave of his happy celebration. Herr Wolff knows only that he is to do as I have said. He knows nothing of you or of your history. Please do not try to enlighten him in any way, it would do no good. After you have met the Führer you may be off and about your business as I will mine." Himmler gave a short smile, clicked his heels in a half bow and left to join Hitler.

The SS lieutenant addressed himself to the sergeant. "You will please stay close to me until after the presentation." Langer grunted his assent. The whole feeling of this was weird, the atmosphere of forced cheer. Most of the ministers had already packed and would be on their way out of Berlin before nightfall. Politicians always covered themselves, and transport was standing in wait for them.

Their loyalty as such to their leader was that they would leave him to face the future alone. Several already had their escape routes out of Germany prepared along with documents giving them citizenship in different countries, though neutral Switzerland was the favorite.

Langer and his escort followed the Führer outside. There Adolf Hitler disappeared for a while inside the entrance to his bunker. Langer and the officer smoked a cigaret during his absence.

There was no conversation. The officer had evidently been ordered to refrain from any familiarity, though he did give his companion a number of questioning looks. Why would the Führer wish to see a common enlisted man from the army at this time? Steeling his mind he mentally disciplined himself for the unspoken infraction of his orders.

An hour passed and Wolff led Langer to the barren garden just outside the bunker, checked his watch, straightened his tunic and stood ready. He butted out his smoke and adjusted the visored cap with the Deathshead and Reich adler insignia.

Hitler made his appearance just as twenty members of the Hitler youth were led into the garden and placed into a single rank. They had come from the fighting in Berlin. The oldest was sixteen, the youngest was thirteen. All of them were children that the state had taken control of when their parents had died or been killed from either the bombings or the Russians. They were from Dresden and Breslau. Hitler wore an ordinary gray coat which looked too large for his stoop-shouldered frame. He moved from one to the other passing out the Order of the Iron Cross. He stopped at one youth and patted the child's cheek with a grandfatherly gesture, sighed deeply and moved on to the next. These were the last of his Thousand-Year Reich. Children called in to fight in the great battle, children who still believed the myth of their leader.

Two of the boys had knocked out Russian tanks with bazookas the day before in the street fighting. Others had manned the barricades and fought the Asiatics of Russia with the ferocity that only those who believe in fairy tales could muster. Killer children died on the streets of Berlin. If they died fast, they did so with the thought that they had served their leader well and died as did the heroes of the Nordic myth. If it took a little longer for them to expire, and the pain was great, they called for their mothers.

Finishing the awards, for the first time, Hitler looked at Langer. For a moment the dullness left his eyes. He motioned for them to follow and reentered the subterranean bunker that served him as his personal haven.

Wolff and Langer followed. The children were led off to return to the battle. All but two would die in the next three days. Eyes watched them as they followed. One of those pairs belonged to Hitler's personal aide, who looked with mistrust at anyone too near his god.

Langer counted the steps down—forty-four. Inside, he could smell the mustiness that all concrete seems to keep forever wet, damp. Passing gray or moldy orange-colored walls, they followed. The fetid mixed smells of urine from backed-up toilets and sweaty uniforms and boots went with them. The hum of a diesel generator droned constantly, stopping only for a second when it was switched over, coughed and restarted.

Normally to go into the bunker one would have to go through an elaborate system of security checks, but Himmler's presence and the assignment to Wolff evidently served as all the authorization Langer needed.

They followed Hitler down the corridors and corners of his labyrinth. They stopped at a small conference room two doors down from Hitler's rooms and obeyed his beckoning finger to enter.

Hitler sat at the far end, his back to the wall. He didn't like people to be behind him.

Hitler had removed his greatcoat and sat in the familiar gray plain coat with the Iron Cross he had won in the First World War on it. He was a definite contrast to the peacock dress of his general staff, in particular, Hermann Göring. By his plainness he understood that he stood out in a crowd of brilliant uniforms and bemedaled chests. He was, as always, a master showman.

But now the play was ending and he was a tired old man. He thanked Wolff and told him to wait down the hall in the guard and switchboard room until he was sent for.

Obersturmführer Wolff clicked his heels and gave the Hitler salute. *"Zum befehl, mein Führer,"* he said, as he obeyed, leaving the two men alone in the small room.

Hitler indicated for Langer to sit at the far end of the conference table.

His eyes foggy, he looked at the man opposite him for some time. His vision had been failing and he had to strain to keep things in focus, particularly in the dim light of the conference room.

"So you are the one we have waited for so long.

"Casca Rufio Longinus, soldier of Imperial Rome, gladiator and mercenary. It's somewhat ironic that you have ended up fighting for the Brotherhood. That's why we lost you for so long. It never occurred to us that you might be on our side in this war." Hitler laughed and coughed, his left hand holding his right to control the trembling in the arm.

"You know, I never really believed the story of you. But here you are. You really exist." Wonder touched the edge of his voice.

"I have naturally read all the reports of your physical description—the scars on your face and wrist. Show me your hands." The thin, ragged, circular scar encircling his left wrist brought a spark to dulled eyes. "It's really true." Hitler glanced at the clock on the wall. "I don't have much time. Tell me what really happened at Golgotha when Jesus died."

Langer spoke, trying to keep himself from strangling the madman. "What do you care about Jesus? I don't understand. He was a Jew, yet you kill Jews as inferior beings. Why should you have any interest?" He deliberately omitted the obligatory title of "Mein Führer" or even sir.

Hitler responded, "You really don't know? It's quite simple. We have definite proof that Jesus was not Jewish. He was of an ancient Aryan stock, the same as the pure blood of the German tribes. Jesus was not a Jew."

Langer laughed. "Then he could have fooled me. He was as Jewish-looking as I ever saw. Not like the paintings of him with light-brown hair and blue eyes. He was a small man with a large Semitic hook nose and bad skin. He was a Jew, but he died well. Will you be able to claim the same"—sarcasm touched at his words—"Mein Führer?"

Hitler refused to rise to the argument. "That you will see for yourself, Herr Longinus. That you will most certainly see for yourself.

"You know, you could do something about all those scars. They have learned some remarkable things about plastic surgery lately. You could have most of them erased." His mind wandered; then with a visible effort he drew himself back. Now he ordered him to tell him about the crucifixion. "I have to know."

Langer hesitated a moment, then decided, why not?

He turned on his mind, letting the past sweep over him, rushing, not conscious of his words as he let the past take over and let Hitler go with him to

198

the Mount of Golgotha. To experience the storm of that hot afternoon, the sweat running down his legs. The priests of the Sanhedrin who came to mock the man on the cross. The moment when the storm was reaching its peak and he struck with his spear into the side of the man they called Messiah. Hitler felt in his words the feel of the Roman uniform, the rubbing of the leather against sore spots, the grating of sand in the sandals, the caligula.

He experienced, in Langer's words, the final moment when Jesus looked on the man who killed him and spoke, the storm around them breaking, the wind screaming. "As you are so you shall remain until I come again."

Hitler wept.

Langer finished, breathed deeply. He didn't like this reliving of his past, it drained him. Hitler wiped his eyes with a linen handkerchief. "It's true, it's all true, you were there." Taking a gulp of air, Hitler composed himself.

Breathing deeply from the emotional exhaustion that had overcome him he spoke, his voice a little stronger than before. "Now I know all our work and sacrifices will not have been in vain. I will not have lived in vain. Everything is clear to me now. Thank you, Herr Longinus, or Langer, whichever you prefer. This moment has given me the will to do what must be done. You are free to go. But return to this place on the thirtieth of April. There will be something happening that you would not want to miss. My death."

Langer rose, facing the maniac. "You bet your ass I will be here. That is one thing you can be certain I want to be present for."

He did an about-face unconsciously and left the room.

Hitler picked up the phone and gave instructions to Wolff, who intercepted Langer in the hallway. "Come with me." He led Langer out of the bunker and back to the chancellery. There he took him to an arms room filled with weapons and equipment.

"Take what you want." He handed him a card. "This will permit your entry into this place and the Führer bunker at any time. You are on your own." He clicked his heels, hailed Hitler and left. Langer looked over the stockpile. The crunch of a Russian heavy shell shook the building.

He picked out one of the new Stg-44 assault rifles. If they only had weapons like this early enough, they could have given Ivan hell. The rifle fired both semi- and fully automatic. The rifle fired a short 7.92. It had a thirty-round magazine, a muzzle velocity of 2,132 feet per second and fired on fully automatic five hundred rounds per minute. A damned fine weapon, better than anything made anywhere else in the world and like most of the things that had come out of German science, too late to do the soldiers in the field any good. Well, he could put it to good use now. Himmler was right about one thing. For once, they had a common enemy, the Russians in the city. Maybe he could do some good there. Taking out as many as he could before the end. But he knew that he would, at any cost, be back at the bunker on the thirtieth. That left him only two days.

Langer picked out a field pack and stuffed it with

loose rounds for the Stg-44, sat down on a crate and filled up ten magazines. These went into two bread bags, one slung from each shoulder. Another sack he filled with egg grenades. They took up less room than the potato masher type. Two canteens and iron rations. Last was a Kar-98 bayonet and a short close-combat knife to fit in his boot top. From a pile of unissued uniforms he picked out one of the canvas material splinter camouflage jackets. It wouldn't help too much in daylight on the streets, but at night the patterns would blend perfectly with dark shadows.

He left the confines of the chancellery and entered the streets of Berlin. Stopping, he listened. It would make no difference which way he went, the enemy was all around them. Refugees were kept out of this area by the SS and police, but in the city itself, he knew they would be huddling in basements and corners seeking shelter in attics. In the subways would be thousands of women, men and children. He checked his weapon, moved across Unter den Linden passing the Brandenburg Gate. From there, he worked his way through the rubble and smoke to Invaliden Strasse. He had passed small groups of men being herded up to the lines. The SS were rounding up deserters and stragglers. Hitler youth and men from the SA and Arbeit Corps. Anyone who could carry a weapon was forced into the line.

From a lamp post where Muller Chaussee intersected the Invaliden, the body of a *Gauleiter* in full uniform swung slowly back and forth. The homemade sign around his once well-fed neck read,

"I hang here because I lost faith in the Führer. So die all defeatists. Heil Hitler."

The crackling of small arms fire told him that he was close to the lines.

When the encirclement was completed there were two million civilians in the confines of the city. On the twenty-sixth, Zhukov came from the north and Koniev from the south, driving their armies on through the defense of the city. Tanks grinding the defenders under after the artillery and rockets first softened up the positions. In two days of hellish fighting the Russian forces under Zhukov had advanced to the Spree. And Koniev had nearly reached the Tiergarten. The two armies were separated by only about two kilometers; the city was nearly cut in half. Between lay the last outpost of Nazi Germany: the Führer bunker.

The mass bombings of the city had nearly stopped. The Americans and the British didn't want to kill any of their Russian allies below. But the Russian artillery took over with massive selective fire barrages that destroyed whole blocks and all in it. Napoleon would have groaned with envy at the numbers of guns used. Between them, Koniev and Zhukov mustered nearly two and a half million men for the battle. But this time the streets were in favor of the defenders and they fought with a ferocity not seen on the front for a long time. He knew this was the final battle, all else mattered not. They had to hold on until the Americans came. Then, the Führer would most certainly ally himself with them and between they would turn against the Russians and drive back to the mud huts and plains from whence they came. Langer knew better. The Americans and Russians might have a go at it later, but not now. There would be no help from the Western Allies. They, too, had a score to settle and were content to let the Russians do their dirty work for them.

He pulled his pack up a little higher and test fired his weapon. The sound of his shots wouldn't be heard against the thunder of the artillery and bursting buildings. Satisfied, he moved out into the streets, taking shelter from building to building. A group of paratroopers from the 9th Airborne Division passed him moving fast and at the ready; they were wearing their peculiar canvas smocks, the pockets bulging with ammo and grenades. Langer followed, keeping a distance between them and himself. In this battle, he preferred to go it alone when he could. Several times parties of roaming SS had tried to impress him along with others into hastily formed battle groups.

The card given him by Wolff changed their minds and they left him alone.

The next days were one of horror. Men and women died by the hundreds and thousands. Russians penetrated into the city in hundreds, riding the backs of tanks shooting at everything that moved, animals and even children. But some of the children fought back and more than one T-34 or heavy Joseph Stalin tank and its crew fell victim to twelve- or thirteen-year-old boys breaking a bottle filled with naphtha, benzine and phosphorous against the steel plating. From the windows and alleys, women who had been repeatedly raped by the Russians in their advance on Silesia and Pomerania finally found revenge firing bazookas and *Panzerfausts;* they killed and were killed. Their vengeance on the Russians taken alive was equal to the treatment they had at the hands of the hordes of Asia.

Bodies littered the streets, many mutilated beyond any recognition by the tracks of tanks and wheels of trucks running over them. There was little time now to bury the dead. They were just hauled into basements, placed in new rows, stacked up and the building blasted down on them to serve as their tomb. Langer hunted his prey eagerly and returned to the chancellery several times to replenish his supplies of ammunition and food, then going back out to fight. Russians died from single shots, slit throats and the garrote. Langer knew all the ways of killing. Several times he had come on one or two Russians separated from their packs and stopping to enjoy themselves with a woman before killing her and hurrying on to catch up with their comrades. These he killed with a special pleasure. They kicked the dead bodies of the women or girls. Children of nine or ten were not too young for the attention of the heroes of the Soviet. Even grandmothers of eighty had their clothes ripped from them and were tossed out open windows to smash against the streets below.

Not all of his victims were Russians. He still took the opportunity when it presented itself to eliminate a squad of SS herding civilians rounded up to be shot for some infraction or another. It was a city gone mad. Women threw themselves from buildings to escape, others became killers and hunters seeking their own salvation in the death of others.

On the twenty-fifth, the forces of the Russian armies completed the encirclement of the city.

The armies of Koniev and Zhukov met on the west side of Berlin. There was no way out now for the civilians to flee. Only small parties managed to slip through now and again. On the same day, regiments of the American army made the first contact with Russian forces on the Elbe River at the city of Torgau.

Uniforms were everywhere, not only those of the army and SS, but also navy and Luftwaffe. He saw several pilots talking together in groups. They had been issued rifles to fight with instead of planes. There was no fuel for the new fighters that continued to turn out on the assembly of Messerschmitt and Fokker. Langer wondered how many would survive the next few days. It was a lot different fighting on the ground. Their courage was not in question, only their experience. Enthusiasm would make little difference to a Mongol with a bayonet at your throat.

He sat down in the shelter of a bombed-out bank. Taking his pack off, he leaned back and shut his eyes. Tonight he would go hunting. It was time now to rest.

The sound of sirens woke him. The high keening wail meant a raid from the RAF was on its way. They usually hit about midnight. The sirens screamed and faded, screamed and faded. Then he heard the droning of hundreds of planes. The burning of the city lighted the way for the British bombardiers at their sights. A few antiaircraft guns fired ineffectually into the sky. Then came the bombs, thousands of the high explosives and incendiaries. The city blazed anew. Whole districts were lit up as bright as day. The only good thing about the bombing was that the Russians wouldn't attack in the target area with ground troops until it was over. People by the hundreds were melted from the intense heat of the fire bombings. Stacked on top of each other in cellars and bomb shelters they just melted. In the mornings special cleanup squads with flame throwers would go through the buildings and burn what was left of the civilians trapped below. Disease was a danger too.

The animals in the zoo were killed and eaten on the twenty-ninth. Most of them, at any rate. Langer gnawed on his iron ration and took a swig of water from his canteen, waiting behind a pile of bricks, the dust coating his face, collecting in the wrinkles by the corners of his eyes. He squinted down Prenzlauer alley.

Across the way he could see a mixed bag of Panzergrenadiers and Hitler youth bring a captured Russian 76 mm antitank gun into position. Only the barrel showed from where he lay. From the street itself the Russians would see nothing. On the rooftops snipers lay in wait. The street had the hell pasted out of it earlier and it was about time for Ivan to come on. These were tough men and even the children had hard eyes in their small faces under oversized helmets, dirty urchin faces hungry for more than food. How could they send the killer children back to the playgrounds and schools after they had experienced this. For them childhood was lost.

They were coming. The distinctive clatter of metal treads against the pavement of the street preceded the actual sight of the tanks. In front were the infantry leaping from door to door in front of their iron escorts, submachine guns at the ready. The defenders held their fire; they wanted tanks. On the rooftops, too, there was sign of the snipers lying in wait. They would hold their fire until the tanks were knocked out and they would go after the infantry. The tanks came rumbling over debris and broken bodies. The JS-1 swung its barrel slowly from side to side, seeking out something to kill, behind it a T-34 and another Stalin. The crew behind the captured 76 waited, the gunners carefully sighting, following the advance of the enemy until they were sure there would be no error in their firing. If they missed they would most likely have little chance of getting off another shot. From his position Langer could see clearly the faces of the gun crew lying in wait, the tension in the clenched jaws. He, too, waited from his cover, sighting on the leader of the Russian advance party. He carefully kept him in his sights, knowing that when the antitank gun fired he had to take out his target quickly. Without leaders the Russians showed very little ability for individual action.

The JS moved closer, the sound of its engine echoing from the side of ruined buildings and offices.

The 76 mm fired, the round hit the side of the

junction between hall and turret, a perfect shot. The JS just stopped. For some reason it didn't explode, but all in it were dead. It just sat there half blocking the street.

With the shot from the 76, Langer fired also a single round aimed for the largest part of the body, the stomach and chest. A pro wasted little on fancy shooting. The idea was to take them out, not to take chances. The Russian doubled over and fell face first to the pavement, his feet kicking as if he were still trying to run. Langer wasted no more time on him; another quick shot, then one more. Two more lay crumpled in the doorways of the city they came to kill.

The sniper on the rooftops opened up. Selectively picking targets, they sent bullets smashing into helmeted heads bursting the brains inside. They had some of the new Kar-44 sniper rifles with scopes and knew damned well how to use them. The Russian tanks tried to raise their guns high enough to fire at the snipers but they couldn't elevate enough, so they just began to fire into the buildings. Round after round until the entire structure would crumble and fall in on itself.

The gun crew reloaded and took out another tank before the Russians spotted it. They lay over its side, the barrel twisted, its crew scattered about in twisted, awkward positions. The child soldiers, two smaller bodies beside the larger, lay looking suddenly even smaller than their actual size. Why did death diminish one so much that even at the instant of dying one always looked smaller? Langer pulled back, there was little more he could do here. He had an appointment tomorrow morning and didn't want to miss it.

Scrambling backwards to keep out of sight, he groped his way through the back of his shelter to the adjoining street, stood in a door where he looked down the street, and got ready to run across. Holding his weapon close to his chest he took a breath and stepped out, only to bump chest first into an equally surprised member of the 1st Guards Army, a veteran of many battles. They both froze for an instant, they were too close to shoot. Arms went around each other's bodies. They held on twisting and grappling, the Russian in his straining grimace showing a full set of stainless steel teeth. He put a leg behind him and twisted Langer down to the pavement, falling. Langer's hand went to his boot. The small, close-combat knife with the wooden handle and short, four-inch blade. He struck again and again five or ten times, but the damned Russian just wouldn't die, he kept trying to crush Langer's throat between his black-nailed hands. Then the body just quit, the life clock stopped. The Russian gave one long sighing shudder and was still. Langer rolled out from under him, his jacket covered with the Russian's blood, recovered his assault rifle and raced down the street to lose himself in the maze of wrecked buildings and alleys.

That final night Langer lay concealed in the ruins of a burned-out apartment building. He found a single mattress to lie on, his eye watching the sky, counting the fiery tails of the rocket barrages from the Katyushas two miles away race through the night like manmade comets.

He wondered what the next day would bring, 30 April 1945. A world was ending, what would the new one bring? Probably more of the same after they had a chance to rest.

He also knew that beneath him in the subways of Berlin thousands also waited for the morning to come. Would the new day bring peace or death? They had no choice. They also waited. Ten days, it seemed much longer.

Things had been busy at the Führer bunker also. Hitler had fired Göring and replaced him with General Baron von Greim. Himmler had been conducting talks with Count Bernnadotte of the Swedish Red Cross, discussing the capitulation of German forces with him as the new head of the German people. Hitler branded him a traitor too. In these final hours he forgot who his master was. Eva Braun's brother, SS General Fegelein was shot for treason that didn't exist this very night. As Langer slept, Hitler married her. Few were left in the bunker now. Most had found one reason or another to absent themselves and never returned. Only a few loyal retainers waited for the end. They had bound their fate to that of his and knew no other way of ending it. They had to see through to the final act before they would be free of their oaths of allegiance.

Langer's sleep was full of twisting, turning dreams that came and went. Tendrils of thought and memories. The dying of a city, a nation and an insane idea lulled him finally to deep, dreamless rest.

* * *

GOTTERDAMMERUNG
April 30, 1945

Hitler moved with the shuffling steps of an old man, his right arm trembling, eyes vacuous, lips pale. He moved down the corridor followed by the last of the royal retainers, stopping before the entrance to his small rooms. Turning, he looked at the faces of those left out of the millions that had so recently worshipped at his altar of the greater German Reich.

Casca stood silently as the Führer shook the hands of the men and patted the cheeks of the women as he sent them away weeping. Even at the end, he had a strange power which aroused great emotions and loyalty from women.

Those left were a poor facsimile of the former glory. Unshaven faces and dingy uniforms from the dust which constantly fell in response to the seemingly unending barrage of Russian shells as the city above them was destroyed. The generator droned on, tended by its loyal retainer. . . .

Bormann, Goebbels, General Burgdorf and Krebs, Linge and Artur Axman who had arrived too late for the midnight wedding of Hitler and Eva and several others were visible at the far ends of the hall—all waiting, expectantly. A world was ending.

Major Guensche moved down the hall closer to the door. Hitler looked at him and smiled gently, wearily. Taking a deep breath, he tried to give his voice some semblance of the former strength it once had when he drove men and women into a fanatical hysteria with the sheer force of his personality.

Pointing with his left hand at Casca, he spoke. "I have one last command. In the name of all that was and all that will be, you must obey. If you have any loyalty to me and our dream, you MUST obey."

His hand wavered with emotion, his voice cracked for a moment and then the spark returned to his dulled eyes. His voice rose, gaining in strength. The listeners straightened and the officers stood to attention. This was their god speaking.

"This man," he said, touching Casca's sleeve, "does not exist. You have never seen him. He has never been here. You may speak of men after this is over, but never, *never must you ever in your lives* —however how long—*never speak of this man*."

Catching another breath, he went on: "When this is over he will leave my rooms. You will not speak to him or question him. He must be left to go his way without delay or hindrance. Do you understand?"

One of the unlookers responded with the force of an old habit, "*Jawohl mein Führer, zum befehl.* Yes, my leader, at your command."

"Good. You will wait ten minutes before entering." Nodding, Hitler indicated for Casca to precede him into his quarters. Eva sat on the far side of the blue and white sofa to the left of the room. Her pleasant face smiled timidly at Casca. Her feet were curled up under her and her shoes lay at the foot of the sofa. At first glance, she looked like an attractive housewife waiting for her husband to come home. In front of her on the sofa table was her pistol, a 6.35 Walther automatic pistol.

Hitler laid two guns on the table, one like Eva's he had carried hidden in a small leather holster sewn into his trousers which he had worn for years and the other a larger caliber, a 7.65 Walther automatic. Sighing, he reached into his coat pocket and removed a small white box and placed it on the table.

With trembling hands, he opened it and took out two poison vials from the half dozen inside. Saying nothing to Eva, he handed her one, which she took as if it were no more than a headache remedy. As she smiled shyly at Casca, he thought how out of place she looked here.

Casca stood silently watching the interplay. His jacket was a little too tight and the room stifling as the diesel generator coughed, missed and then settled back into its steady drone. Hitler sat on the left side of the sofa, running his fingers through his hair, looking into the emotionless face of the man standing before him, "Longinus, the reason you are here with me at this moment is simple. Germany is dying and in a few moments I will join her—I and my wife," as he acknowledged Eva's presence for the first time. "We die, but you go on through the years and centuries. This moment must not be completely lost to history. When you leave here, only you will know the truth and bear witness to my sacrifice as you did to that of Jesus. He, too, came to save the world and died for it as I die for my world. As Jesus died and found greater order with his death, so my followers shall; even now hundreds are already preparing for he who shall come after me. I have shown the way. Now it is for the others to take up my work where I leave off. Like you, the brotherhood lives. Now it is time for you to witness my crucifixion in this subterranean Golgotha."

Turning to Eva, he spoke gently, as he would to a child. "You are to go with me. I would not have you treated badly or put on display for the mob to gawk at." He patted her hand. "Now, it is time."

Eva smiled, her round face childlike in its faith. She placed the vial of potassium cyanide between her teeth as did Hitler. The Führer nodded at her as he placed his own vial between his front teeth. Eva bit down and the smell of bitter almonds filled the small enclosure, as her body gave one short shudder. She died, her feet still curled under her, looking as if she had fallen asleep on the sofa after coming home from a dinner with friends in the pleasant hills of Bavaria.

Hitler did not bite down. He trembled, still holding the vial between his teeth as he looked first at Eva and then back at Casca. Raising his face, he spoke, the deadly vial between his teeth, as his courage wavered. He spoke to the man of the centuries: "You will tell the future of me?"

With a smooth upward sweep of his hand, Casca slapped the Führer's jaw shut, splintering the glass vial and sending the poison into Hitler's mouth. As the Führer trembled in his death, Casca spoke for the first time: "No."

Reaching over, Casca picked the Walther up from the table and put one bullet into the head of this holy German messiah. The smell of the cordite mingled with that of the poison; he dropped the gun beside the body of Hitler, and it fell to the carpet. Casca had been inside the room three minutes.

He gave the room one last look. Moving to the body of Eva, he pulled her skirt down to cover an expanse of thigh. Whatever she was, she had the courage to die—more than the man she loved. Opening the sealed double doors, Casca stepped into the hall, closing the door behind him. The waiters heard nothing; fireproof and gas-proof doors prevented this. Casca merely nodded and turned right, heading to the supply room to collect his gear. The faces of those waiting were pale, frightened and confused, but no questions were asked and nothing was volunteered. They would wait the prescribed ten minutes. The only sound was that of his boots slapping against the concrete floor and the droning generator.

Gathering up his gear, Casca slung his pack to his back and picked up one of the new Stg-44 assault rifles that fired the 7.92 Kurz round and headed out down the passageway that led to the chancellery. Those who still had the strength were involved in an orgy of desperation. Women who had been fleeing the Russians gave themselves to any soldier who would have them, while in the makeshift hospital, Professor Schenek amputated the leg of a fourteen-year-old Hitler youth who had blown his own leg off when he tried to knock out a T-34 with a sticky bomb. The boy died before the leg could be tossed into the trash with the others.

Casca hunched low, waiting his chance. Dawn would soon be on him and he had to move quickly. To be caught in the light would certainly mean capture. The sound of Russians under the bridge was broken by a short round from one of their own 105 mms that blasted several men to bits and sent the others to the ground for cover.

Casca raced across the bridge, bending low to the ground, his assault rifle at the ready. On the opposite end of the bridge a scared Mongolian-looking face raised up from behind a pile of rubble in time to be shot through the mouth by a short three-round burst from the Stg-44. Leaping over the body, Casca ran into a cloud of smoke and entered hell. . . .

He stood in the midst of an inferno. Buildings on both sides of the street were burning fiercely. The intensity of the fires made whirlwinds of flames dance and the heat tried to suck the air from his lungs. Acrid clouds of yellow smoke whirled and twisted as buildings crumpled, throwing clouds of ashes, sucked up by the flames and spread over the city.

Casca stood frozen in the halo of the flames raging about him as gray ash with small red sparks of life tried to catch his clothing on fire so that he too could become part of the holocaust. Ashes covering his face and mouth were the same dull color of the ground now three inches deep with ashes. In front of him halfway down the block, a four-storied apartment building's brick exterior crumbled and fell away, leaving only a burning frame. Katyushas added their own special sound to this overture of destruction with an intensity that would have made Wagner pale. As the framework of the building was consumed in clouds of yellow smoke, one part of the structure remained. Three stories high, it blazed and all ·that was left was a giant burning cross, wrapped in dancing licking flames, reaching for the heavens then wrapping around itself lovingly, feeding the raging roar and blast, making tears run down his face, cutting clean small channels that showed skin beneath the coatings of ash and dust. The structure burned until all that was left was a giant cross.

Watching fascinated through watering, burning eyes, Casca looked into the fires of Götterdämmerung. For a fleeting moment, a face looked out from the fire of the burning cross, gentle eyes in a sad face as the smoke formed a wreath of thorns and then it was gone.

Numbly, Casca blinked. His throat was dry and cracking as soundless words came through the maelstrom of the inferno. . . .

"Nothing changes. All that was will be. The wheel turns once more."

The square back of the soldier hunched over as he walked into the cloud of twisting yellow and red smoke, the flames kissing his boots as the clouds covered him and the cross crumbled into ash.

Goldman shook his head. Things began to come back into focus. A doorman standing erect at his position looked at him with a concerned expression.

"Are you all right, sir?" He spoke in English, recognizing the American cut of his clothes. "May I call a doctor?"

Goldman looked about him. Casca was gone, vanished in the afternoon crowd. "No, no, I'm quite all right, thank you. Just a touch of dizziness."

He left the doorman still looking after him and walked out onto the crowded sidewalks. Evening was near, the lights of the city were coming on to signal another carefree night of gaiety.

Where are you now, Casca? Why have you chosen me to do this to? I don't want it but I can't stop it. I know sometime somewhere you'll come again and I'll be waiting. Till then, auf Wiedersehen, *you miserable bastard. I think I've said that before.*

Carl Langer was waiting in line at the airport at Templehof. The announcer gave the departures over the PA in German, French and English. Flights going all over the world.

The plane to the Orient wouldn't be leaving for a couple of hours yet. He paid for his ticket and found a seat to wait in. He had time to kill. Yes, that was one thing he always had plenty of. Time.